MW01435652

No longer property of the
Dayton & Montgomery County Public Library

Westwood Branch Library

Sherbourne's Folly

Sherbourne's Folly

NORA BARRY

PUBLISHED FOR THE CRIME CLUB BY
DOUBLEDAY & COMPANY, INC.
GARDEN CITY, NEW YORK
1978

All of the characters in this book are fictitious, and any resemblance to actual persons, living or dead, is purely coincidental.

First Edition

ISBN: 0-385-12882-7
Library of Congress Catalog Card Number 77-76220
Copyright © 1978 by Doubleday & Company, Inc.
All Rights Reserved
Printed in the United States of America

For
B.W.C., N.C., C.J.H., *and* J.P.F.
with love

Sherbourne's Folly

CHAPTER 1

It was odd, to be going home again. Ten years ago I had flown the Atlantic, taken this same train from London and known that I was old enough to die. Married, with a daughter, it had taken my father's death to bring recognition of my own mortality; a jolting into maturity. It seemed the end of home, of a place to go where everything would be all right, a last resort of unquestioning comfort.

And now I was going home again, perhaps to another death. And with me my now grown-up daughter. *Going home, going home.* The wheels of the train against the tracks pounded their rhythm into my mind. Going home to Snowsdown, to the scenes and memories and moments that could fade for long periods of time only to be thrust into my consciousness by a familiar word or tone, by the lean of a tree suddenly caught in my vision. Going home to that place in my mind, home to Snowsdown.

Snowsdown Manor, an unpretentious house lying in the heart of England, the Vale of Evesham. A Warwickshire house built from the natural stone of its quarries, designed to sit upon the rich land, to blend with the rolling hills. I thought it—and my childhood—gone when Father died. But Monica had been there, controlling, holding us all together. The focus as, in fact, she'd always been.

Jennifer was on the seat opposite, straining against the

window as she tried to see beyond the lights of our compartment into the dark countryside. She had been quiet since boarding the train in London over an hour ago; perhaps she sensed my mood, perhaps she was anxious to see the countryside she'd heard so much about. She looked tired, her fine, dark hair straggled across her shoulders, catching the light in moments as the bare bulbs above us shook and the train swayed around us.

"Do you think Aunt Monica is dying?" she asked, suddenly turning from the window to look at me. She caught me staring. "Don't worry, Mother, I'll make it to Snowsdown. I won't pass out on you."

I smiled and felt like crying. I was more tired than I'd thought, more disturbed and confused than I'd known. Yesterday was a spring afternoon in Connecticut, today a long nightmare of frantic travel to see my sister who was ill. Connecticut was little more than three thousand miles away; at that moment it might have been three thousand light years. Disassociated by the grueling hours of changed plans and hurried travel, my life seemed connected only to this train beating its way through the English countryside.

Come soon, it said. *Monica not at all well. Not desperate, but advance your plans if possible. Roger.* We had been in the garden when the telegram arrived, John, Jennifer and I. We dropped everything, made new arrangements and left. John was still at home—he had another two weeks to teach. Our plans had called for all of us to come together next month.

"I don't know, darling." Monica's husband was a practical, calm man, but I was scared and tried to keep my voice steady. "Roger did say it wasn't desperate, but then he wouldn't have sent a telegram if there wasn't some urgency." We didn't know what we'd find.

Contact for a moment comfortingly made, Jennifer returned to the blackness of the window and the occasional cluster of lights which sped past us. Snowsdown, home, had been a special trip planned by all of us, partly a graduation gift for Jennifer, partly for the three of us to be with my English family. A last time for John and I to be with Jennifer before she went off to her own life. A time together, to be father, mother and daughter, to act the roles we all knew so well, were at ease with.

Another hour. I could hear the porter's voice working its way down the corridor, "Last call for the dining car, last call for the dining car." He opened our compartment door to make his announcement directly and with him came the sounds and quiet, the eeriness and isolation of night travel. The door closed as quickly and we were back in our own silence.

"Will we be met, do you think, Mother?"

"I imagine so." I looked at my watch, almost midnight. "There won't be many taxis around at this time of night, and it's almost fifteen miles to Lower Pershing from Evesham. Probably Marcus or Roger will come."

I had sent a telegram giving Roger the time of arrival and flight number. Of course, there was no way anyone could know what train we would be on from London. But this was the last one. I hoped we'd be met; I felt too tired, inadequate to deal with the trauma of finding a taxi, of waiting for it to come and then giving directions to Lower Pershing and Snowsdown.

"What's he like, Mother?"

"Who? Roger or Marcus?"

"Marcus, of course. I know what Uncle Roger's like. He did visit us."

"You were only little then."

"But I was entranced by him. Don't you remember, I hid his hat to keep him from leaving."

I smiled, seeing Roger's frantic search. Jennifer had stared at him all weekend. She couldn't understand most of what he said, his voice was fast and flew in a different cadence than those she knew in Connecticut. He had tried, in his awkward, gentle way, to be kind to his small niece. He'd told her about the family dogs.

"I must have made him uncomfortable," she said now, "but he seemed very exotic to me then. But it's Marcus I want to know about. What's he like? You're close in age, aren't you?"

"Yes, we are," I said. "So is Willow. Monica's the oldest one."

We were really two separate families. Monica was our half sister. Her mother, Father's first wife, died when she was born and Monica was raised by nurses and nannies until Father married again fifteen years later.

"Monica was too old to be a sister." I smiled. "She was more like our mother."

Marcus was the youngest, a little boy with three sisters, two of them only a year or two older than he, had been spoiled, but he grew up to be a dashing young man. Tall and blond, good looking in a solid way.

"He used to drive a red MG," I told her. "There was a girl in the village who adored him. She would wait for the two o'clock bus to Evesham on Saturday afternoons. I know she used to hope Marcus would come by in the MG before the bus came. Sometimes he did, pulling up beside her, brakes squealing, motor revving. 'Hop in,' he'd shout above the roar. And off they'd go, never speaking to each other or seeing each other beyond the ride."

"Well, didn't he like her much? Who was she?" asked Jennifer.

"A village girl he liked to dazzle. We used to tease him about it, saying she was really interested in MGs. He was very embarrassed by it all, and I imagine he's still like that, a big, handsome, shy man."

"Does he like Monica? Do you?" she asked then.

The train was pulling into Evesham Station and I didn't try to sort my feelings for Monica, the giant in my life. In all of our lives. A brilliant, domineering, stubborn, charming, flamboyant woman. The kind you adore to know, love to tell stories about, but at times wished belonged to another family. A perfect friend. Not the sister, guardian, who had influenced and tried to direct your whole life. I at least had gone away to America, but Marcus and Willow had spent their whole lives surrounded by her.

We were alone on the platform, station locked, train gone. A single lamp swung above, casting dim, narrow light into the cool of the early May evening. It hadn't changed at all. Evesham, a bustling town of reasonable population, closed for the night. Worries of finding a phone abandoned my thoughts as we heard a car drive up, the slam of its door, the crunch of footsteps on the gravel parking lot behind the station house.

It was Marcus, tall and flustered, coming toward us. "Sorry, Allison," he called. The light caught his face as he neared and I saw that he'd changed very little in the last few years. It was the brother I remembered, the same ruddy face showing an outdoors life, a shock of light hair across his forehead, and an old tweed jacket. He caught my hand, brushed my cheek with his and quickly gathered our suitcases under his arms and into his hands. He grinned at Jennifer saying it was about time he got to meet his niece. "Do you play that thing?" he asked, nodding toward the guitar she'd insisted on bringing with her, now clutched in her hand. She didn't answer and we stumbled after his back into the dark.

"Careful. Ridiculous. No light anywhere," he mumbled, leading us away from the dingy station. "Follow me. Car's just over here."

He opened the doors, storing the luggage and hurrying us into the warmth. An older Marcus after all; not the MG but a sedate Mercedes coupe. Jennifer climbed into the back with her guitar and I sat beside Marcus with his rambling conversation. "It's cold, are you warm enough? Roger shouldn't have rushed you like this. Monica's going to be all right. Damn town, no signs, no lights." He talked on, expecting no response, uncomfortable for the moment with his sister who was a stranger and the niece he'd never seen before. Our contact for twenty-two years had been slight; I remembered him as a teen-ager, he knew me as an older sister who was always telling him what to do.

"What do you mean, Monica's going to be all right?" I asked. "Roger's telegram sounded urgent. What happened, tell me?"

"Roger's upset. Only natural. Monica had a nasty fall. She's still doing crazy things as if she was twenty-five."

He was wrong. Monica never did crazy things: exotic, exciting, active, interesting things, yes. She'd always had a lot of energy, too many interests, her profession, the family, and her time was carefully structured to encompass everything. No movement, no idea, no journey wasted. Monica was above everything a skilled accomplisher. Exhausting to watch in action, but all that motion, to her, was being alive.

"Sixty's not that old, you know, Roger. What did she fall from? Is she in hospital, at home?"

"No, no, she's not in hospital, she's home carrying on as usual. Willow came down, you know. But she's at a loss—Monica won't take her ministrations."

"But what happened?" I persisted.

"It happened out at the Folly last week. She's had the place repaired, been cleaning it up herself." He looked at me and smiled as he talked of the Folly, our childhood bond. "She was on top of a ladder pulling cobwebs from the ceiling. She said she got dizzy and fell."

"Did she break something? What *is* the matter with her?" I couldn't understand—if Monica was not desperately ill then why had we been called to come so suddenly?

"Old Wyndham thinks she had a slight heart attack when she fell; she's still a bit shaky at times, tires easily. Other than that she's a bit bruised and sore. I gathered things have been worrying her recently too, and Wyndham puts it all down to pressure. Mucking out the Folly was just too much. She won't go to Birmingham or London to see anybody else. Wyndham's going to bring somebody up to see her."

Marcus handled the car well; we were almost home. We

sank back into silence and concentrated on the road before us. Jennifer roused from the back seat to ask what on earth the Folly was. Exhaustion thick in her voice, she was nearly asleep and I didn't answer.

Ask anyone within a twenty mile radius of Lower Pershing for directions to Snowsdown Manor and the chances are no one will know. Ask for Sherbourne's Folly, and they'll put you on the right road to Snowsdown and probably add the complete history of the house and the families who've lived there since 1605.

Walter Sherbourne, for all practical reasons the founder of our family, bought Snowsdown in 1801. He wanted to make it his, found his own great family and eradicate the memory of the one that came before: a landmark, a monument of some kind. He built a replica of the Parthenon—a Folly—in the middle of the maze, which is Snowsdown's real claim to distinction.

Some of the happiest childhood times for Marcus, Willow and I had been spent in the Folly. It was at some distance from the house and we couldn't readily be called away. It was a good walk to the center of the maze, and if the paths weren't cleared regularly, it became even less accessible. It was one room surrounded by columns; a funny, safe place to be. Two sides were open to the breezes—yet it was sheltered and dry—an open room to play or while away an afternoon doing nothing.

We were almost home. Lower Pershing was dark, the headlights of the car showing only the tree-lined streets, the village green and the sign of The Bell as we swept by. Leaving the center of the village the car twisted up the long road to Snowsdown. I caught sight of the house lights through the trees and turned to wake Jennifer. I left the limbo of travel and suddenly felt glad.

Before Jennifer was properly awake, Willow and Roger, dogs surging around their feet, were at the car. I stumbled out to be met by Roger's exuberance. Caught in his bear hug, I relaxed for a moment, savoring the feeling, the smell of my family represented by my elderly brother-in-law's broad chest.

"Dearest Roger, how good it is to be home." I hugged him tightly, startling him with my sudden intensity. He pulled away and I laughed up at him. "It's all right, Roger, I won't eat you. But it's good to be here."

The dogs were jumping at me, friendly and happy. I fought my way out of their pleasure and turned to my younger sister, Willow. She leaned toward me and our cheeks touched. "How quickly you came, I had no idea," she murmured. People didn't change much and Willow's life was still probably confined by London and Lower Pershing. A trip for Willow needs extensive preparation. I imagined her periodic trips to the Continent with Clive, a nightmare of organization. It was good to see and feel us all together.

I attempted to make introductions for Jennifer; we laughed at the formality and straggled on into the house, the dogs barking and romping ahead of us. The lights in the entrance hall were momentarily blinding, but Willow turned the main ones off as we moved into the drawing room. Nothing was changed, I was home and everything looked to be in its place. I moved around, touching remembered objects, running my hand against the fabrics of chairs, the wood of tables and cupboards.

"It's all here, Allison," said Willow. "You can take your coat off."

Jennifer was wide awake again, shy but unable to control her broad smile. "It's just as you described, Mother. Exactly the way you said it would be," satisfaction in her voice.

Willow was staring at her with a look of surprise. For a moment I wondered why and then realized, with some embarrassment, that Willow was horrified by Jennifer's clothes. Faded jeans, jacket and desert boots might be fashionable at Antioch, but they obviously weren't at Snowsdown. I felt like giggling as I watched the amazement cross Willow's face, her efforts to control displeasure at the travel-weary apparition of my daughter before her. Defiance and color flooded Jennifer's face, but she took control and went on. "Mother's talked about this house so much, told family stories, it doesn't feel strange at all."

Roger fetched drinks and we sat suddenly quiet, looking at each other, seeing the passage of time. Hair completely gray now, Roger's face still had that gentle vagueness I'd always found so appealing. He was a big, country-looking man. Big feet, big hands and an inherent elegance that had nothing to do with worldly things.

"Where is everyone, Aunt Willow?" asked Jennifer. "Who else is here?"

"They're all in bed. Monica goes early now. Clive came down from London today too," she said looking over at me. Clive, as I recalled, was a little pompous and did something in The City. I didn't know him well.

Willow, from time to time, was smug. I'd forgotten that. It's strange how time and distance distort things. Willow was once a pretty woman, but age had come early to her. Only forty-one, she already looked matronly, her body set into its ways. Her blond hair had lost some of its luster; she looked faded, but in a fashionable way. A light blue twin set and gray skirt matched perfectly her faded prettiness. As young girls we had been close, a guild of two against Dragon Monica, probably our strongest tie.

"Caroline and Colin are in bed too," she said. Turning to Jennifer and seeing her weariness she offered to take her to her room. Jennifer seemed grateful and relieved. She kissed me good night and they went off together, Marcus trailing with our luggage.

He really hadn't changed. Still that tall, shy, handsome man. I liked him and fleetingly recalled the days when I'd adored him, following him everywhere, embarrassing him with my persistence for attention. When we'd both been very little he'd made me walk everywhere ten paces behind him. And I, older but smaller, did.

"Tell me about Monica, Roger. Why did you send the telegram? Marcus said it's not serious, but your telegram was so urgent."

Roger got up to freshen our drinks. As he crossed the room I noticed for the first time that he too had aged, he was an old man. Perhaps it was just the hour, weariness and worry. "I probably can't tell you much beyond what Marcus already has. Monica fell off the stepladder and seems to have suffered a slight heart attack. She's undergone tests with Wyndham. A specialist is coming up from London, and we should know more very soon."

"But there must be more. Why the urgency of the telegram?"

"I wanted you and Jennifer here. No," he shook his head, "Monica wanted you here. She seemed anxious that it be now. 'I don't want to wait another month,' she said. 'Make them come now.' So I did."

I was too tired to be irritated at their thoughtlessness, selfishness in rushing us here. Suddenly I was very, very weary, upset about Monica and confused.

"And then I started to think about it too," he said. "It seemed right that you should be here now, not in two weeks. Everyone else is—Willow and Clive and Caroline; Colin's just up from Oxford; even old Cartwright's nephew, Nicholas, is here for the summer."

Carrington Cartwright was our nearest neighbor. A charming man whose daughter, Eleanor, was engaged to marry Marcus. It had been a long engagement—several years—and none of us knew when they would marry.

Roger stood up, leaning to tap his pipe out into the dead fire. "I wanted to make this a perfect summer. We haven't been here together since your father's funeral and it seemed right to make it a special summer for Monica, to have you all here again."

"But are you really worried about this accident, Roger? What else is there? You seem puzzled about something."

He looked vaguely beyond me toward the darkness of the french doors and the garden outside. "I think Monica's anxiety about getting you and Jennifer here got through to me. Her insistence puzzles and worries me. I don't understand what it is, but Monica seemed desperate to have you both here, and now."

It didn't sound like Monica; she wasn't given to irrational behavior. She always asked to be adored but never to be idly indulged. I didn't understand either. Had the accident frightened her, shown her the specter of death? Somehow, though, that wouldn't scare Monica. She'd meet death head on as she had life.

We were silent when Willow came quietly back into the room. "Jennifer's already asleep." She was bearing a tea tray; things didn't change much, especially comforting things. One of Willow's unvarying rituals was tea before bed. "Marcus went off to bed too." She began to lay out three cups and saucers. "Will either of you have tea? No, I suppose you're happier with your whisky." I could have sworn she sniffed.

"How old is Caroline now?" I asked her. "Very close to Jennifer, isn't she?"

Willow's face opened. "A little younger, nineteen," she said. "That year in France did her a world of good, gave her a style I can't explain, but it's an amazing change." She smiled and I thought of Jennifer's blue jeans. "Forgive me, but I can't help boasting." Willow was, for a moment, embarrassed by her praise of Caroline. "That I gave birth to that creature is beyond my imagination."

This was more as I knew her; Willow always shy and proud about something, as if she had a secret she was dying to share with us but wouldn't. I loved her best this way.

She turned for Roger's opinion.

"Good-looking girl," he said. "Actually quite stunning."

Willow picked up speed and energy from my silence. I gathered that Caroline was perfect and that Willow had great ambition for her: to marry well, preferably someone with money and possibly even a title. No mention of Caroline's dreams and ambitions. I didn't listen too closely but tuned in as she said ". . . doesn't feel comfortable here," and saw her pulling her shoulders around herself as she sipped her tea.

"What do you mean, she isn't comfortable here," I asked.

"Monica doesn't like her," said Willow with some bitterness.

"Now that's not true, you know it isn't," cried Roger, jumping to defend Monica. "She gets impatient with the girl sometimes, but that doesn't mean she doesn't love to have her here. You know she's not comfortable showing affection."

"You're avoiding me, Roger," said Willow with rare astuteness. "She doesn't like Caroline, always shutting her up, pushing her aside, never listening. And Caroline tries. She adores her Aunt Monica. It's not fair."

Willow's voice had risen, she was almost shouting, her face flushed with anger. "Why she cares more for Carrington's nephew than she does for Caroline."

Suddenly embarrassed she stopped her tirade at Roger, at everything. He went toward her, putting his arm across her shoulders. "You know what it is, Willow," he said kindly. "Monica recognizes too much of herself in Caroline. You know how confused and disturbed we've all been by Monica's tantrums. God knows she's not easy to live with. Caroline's too strong, too beautiful and Monica knows it isn't always the easiest way to live."

It was a new concept for Willow, not an entirely displeasing one. She kissed Roger's cheek and caught my hand, asking us to forgive her weariness. Gathering teacups and tray, she went off to bed.

Roger and I sat quietly for a moment before he said, "She's right, you know, in a way. Monica gets impatient with what she calls Caroline's pretensions. She can be a bit hard on the girl."

"Willow's tired," I said. "Upset, protective and probably blowing it out of proportion."

Roger agreed, we were all tired. Soon we parted and I went up to my own room. No need to be told where it was, to be led there. It was my room, my bed and for a moment I felt like a girl again. The bannister under my hand felt as it always had, each tread of the stairs fit my feet, the gloom of the first floor landing and the doors on either side were all familiar, welcoming. And my door. There was a coal fire burning slowly in the grate, the lights were low and my favorite plaid eiderdown was turned to the bottom of the bed. I walked across to the windows and flung them open. The cool evening air flooded in blowing the white lace curtains aside as I leaned out into the night and felt that I was home.

CHAPTER 2

It was late when I woke; the sun was high and the shadows of the gnarled old apple tree outside the window were moving into the room as the morning wore on. I was home and the warmth of the bed felt familiar, as if I'd never been away. What strangeness, how irrelevant time and events seemed. It had been more than twenty years since I'd lived in this house, called this room mine, and yet I knew if I let it all wash over me, those years away would disappear. Under my bed would be a suitcase full of letters from friends and beaux, badges from the girl guides, report cards, chocolate boxes from long-ago evenings with young men, pressed flowers, the silver cup won swimming at school. Over there in the dressing table drawers would be a shell collection and stamp album, a clutter of bottles growing moldy from too little use.

The curtains were blowing on the breeze drifting through the open windows, and I could smell the green freshness of the gardens, see the pale blue of the sky as I lay there in bed, feeling no different, for a moment, than I had twenty or more years ago.

Time came pressing in with a knock at the door, I called to come in and Jennifer burst, glowing, into the room. I was a mother, I had lived twenty-two years crammed with life that had nothing to do with Snowsdown. I was married to

John and had a home in Connecticut. Snowsdown Manor wasn't home anymore, it was a memory of another, younger me. I was already uneasy about our return, annoyed that we'd been rushed unnecessarily, and I desperately wanted the memory to remain a glad one, wanted a little piece of me to always yearn for this place. I swung out of bed and reached for a robe.

"Good morning, darling. Is everyone up? Am I the only layabout?" I asked her.

"I don't know about layabouts, but there's no sign of aunts Willow and Monica or uncles Clive and Marcus," she rattled their names quickly. Jennifer moved about the room looking at pictures and objects on shelves, the books I'd read as a child and young woman. "This house is marvelous, Mother. I had no idea of its grandness, all the interesting corners, there's lots to explore. You never told me it was this way." Jennifer was excited, surprised by the freshness that age could show, the light of it all. I smiled, remembering that once upon a time I would leap out of bed to run downstairs, singing to greet the day.

"I did meet Colin and Caroline," she said, a somber note suddenly in her voice.

"Oh?"

"I think I might like Colin, he was friendly. And he's very good looking."

"Wasn't Caroline friendly?" I asked thinking ahead to possible problems with Willow and her daughter.

"Well, she hardly said good morning. She didn't introduce herself, I was just supposed to *know* who she was. I got the feeling she wasn't too keen having me around. She's a condescending bitch."

Unusual for Jennifer to talk that way. "It's not fair to talk that way about her, Jennifer. You've only met her once. She could be shy and awkward, you know," I placated and reprimanded.

"Maybe, but I doubt it. It was all very uncomfortable. She announced she and Colin were going to ride over at Cartwright's this afternoon; apparently they keep their own horses over there. Colin just went along with it all."

"Eleanor keeps a stable," I said. "She gives lessons and boards some local horses. I understand she's rather good. You could go over with them, you know. I'm sure you could borrow or rent a horse from her."

"But Mother, I wasn't *invited*," wailed Jennifer. "I just don't feel good about it all."

I was disturbed to hear that Caroline had been less than friendly. If all that Willow said about her daughter was true, if she was mature and stylish, Jennifer might be in for a rough time. I hoped it wasn't going to become a problem. I didn't like to think of Roger's plans for a peaceful family summer being destroyed by petty squabbling.

"There's another thing too," she said looking embarrassed. "I asked if there were any ghosts at Snowsdown." She looked at me defiantly as my face moved to smile. "Well, it's a reasonable question, it's an old house. Besides, I felt as if someone or something was in my room last night."

"What do you mean?" I asked. "What on earth happened?"

She moved to sit on the edge of my unmade bed, her expression puzzled. "Well, it's all a bit hazy—almost like a dream, hard to know what's real and what isn't. Anyway, one moment I was fast asleep and in the next something woke me up. Something warned me that things weren't right."

Although Jennifer was now sprawled across the bed in an illusion of ease, she was looking at me intently, willing me to believe her story. "There was a shadowy figure at the bottom of my bed. I couldn't see clearly, my eyes weren't adjusted to the light coming through the window, but something was there and it moved. I struggled to wake up properly, to focus my eyes, and by the time I was out of bed the vision had just disappeared."

I was sitting at the dressing table mirror, combing my hair, and I could see Jennifer's reflection in front of me. Something had disturbed her. I doubted it was ghosts.

"There aren't any ghosts at Snowsdown, Jennifer," I said calmly. "Not even any local legends—at least none that we've heard."

"Well, something happened. I was frightened by something. I even opened the door and looked down the corridor."

"And you didn't see anything, did you?" I asked.

She shook her head and I continued. "You were exhausted, you know, and excited. All those stories I've been telling you for years about the house and family were probably surging around your subconscious and giving you nightmares." I dismissed her fears, remembering some of the nightmares I'd had from time to time in strange places.

She looked relieved for a moment and said, "You're probably right. The thing is, I told Caroline and Colin about it. Caroline *laughed* at me and said I was ridiculous if I believed in ghosts."

So that was it. Caroline was what was worrying Jennifer, not the thought of ghosts and nightmares.

"Colin's possible," Jennifer said looking brighter. "I shall just have to work on him." She smiled. "Lessen the impact of Cousin Caroline. He's tall and fair like everyone else in this family," she mused. "Do you realize that I'm the only one here who isn't tall and blonde?"

"It's strange," she continued slowly, "it makes me realize, perhaps for the very first time, that I'm not really part of this family at all."

I put down the comb and moved to sit beside her on the bed, giving her a gentle hug. "But you are. You're my daughter, mine and John's. It has nothing to do with where you were born. You've never felt you didn't belong before. Coming here should change none of that."

"But you chose me, the rest of the family didn't," a troubled, disconcerted frown passed her face.

"They will, darling, they will." We both stood and she moved to the door. "Go down now, and let me bathe. I'll join you soon. Perhaps you'll take a walk around with me. I'm dying to walk through the maze, into the Folly again."

She left, and I moved slowly to get ready for the day. I hadn't thought at all about the impact of my family on Jennifer, about hers on them. All so linked, in my mind, it was sometimes hard to remember that they didn't know each other, that I was only a link in their meeting. I rarely thought about having adopted Jennifer. And why should I? She was our daughter, we had nourished and loved her. What difference? Could my love as a mother for a daughter have been greater if I'd carried her in my womb for nine months before letting her out into the world? What were the differences or intensities of love? I shrugged off my melancholic mood. Jennifer was my daughter and I knew that love with the surety that I knew the feel of the bed I'd slept in for more than twenty years and woken in this morning as if they had been yesterday. I was Allison Sherbourne Van Dyck married to John Van Dyck visiting my family home with our daughter, Jennifer. I went down to breakfast with confident steps.

"The daffodils are in bloom, Allison, and I have been waiting a long time for you to come and enjoy them with me again." Monica's voice pierced and floated in its distinctive way from another room. "A vision in blue denim, which I presume to be your daughter, is planted on the lawn, arms akimbo, feet apart, gazing at this house with amazing intensity. Is she interested in architectural detail or planning exercise? Or is it merely her style?"

I called out to the voice, "Am I supposed to guess? It's Margaret Mead or Katharine Hepburn?"

Monica swept, laughing, into the dining room, a woman tall, slender and amused. "As ridiculous as ever, Monica," I laughed with her and moved to embrace her. "Oh, it's good to see you," I said. "I've missed you."

Given to flamboyance only in speech and manner, Monica pulled smoothly away after allowing, for a moment, my embrace. Impossible, frustrating woman. Unfair, Allison, unfair. She'd had her own life to live yet she had always been hampered by her impossible younger sisters and brother demanding her attention, her time, and never enough of either to please us.

She hadn't changed much. Grander. Thinner. Still elegant in a way few people are. Perhaps it was the textures she chose, gentle fabrics that flowed with her. She moved to the sideboard for toast and coffee and as she did I could still see the younger Monica, the prominent archeologist dashing around the world to conferences and digs, lecturing; the television personality, the dominating, stubborn older sister, the charismatic friend.

"Since when did we ever enjoy the daffodils together?" I asked.

"Oh, but we did. I just never told you about it." She looked at me for a moment before turning again to the sideboard and coffee. "You know I love daffodils—they mean spring and new things, new digs and old friends. Snowsdown has more daffodils than any place I've ever seen, and they mean you, Marcus, Willow, Roger. Home." Uneasy with affection or nostalgia, her voice was quiet, almost directed not to me, but to herself. "You are all, with the daffodils, caught inextricably together in my thoughts."

Monica sat down at the table. We both turned slightly to look out of the french doors open to the garden and rolling countryside of Warwickshire. Spring in England. After all the years away the uniqueness, its absolute lightness, the smell of it all, never faded. We had sat here many times, Monica and I, coffee before us, conversation in mind. It was the place for serious conversation, for all of us; the dining table, the garden. For some reason the drawing room, library, study and bedrooms were either too communal or too private, but this room offered the formality serious conversation required. It was here twenty-two years ago that I sat with Monica and told her I wanted to marry

John but was frightened by America. She told me then that nothing was irrevocable.

She *had* aged, her skin was paler, almost translucent and she was too thin. Always before she'd looked years younger than she actually was, but now at sixty, she looked her age.

I had been staring at her. For a moment she glared at me and with some roughness to her voice said, "Don't worry about me, Allison. Don't haunt me with your pity or your nostalgia for times past. Summer is about to begin." For a moment she looked earnest, almost pleading, "I want it to be a good one, it's important to me."

I struggled to deny my pity, to utter some platitude in the guise of comfort, but she continued quietly, raising her hand slightly to stop my voice. "No, no. Don't say anything. I shall tell you."

"Haven't you always?" I tried levity, but couldn't quite smile.

"I am going to die, perhaps next month, perhaps in three. I have leukemia.

"Stay exactly where you are," she commanded in her coolest voice. My breath was caught in the back of my throat, I couldn't speak and was about to reach out.

Not a slight fall, not a mild heart attack, not irrevocable. She sat sipping her coffee and I, stunned, sipped mine with her. This was the moment dreaded when the telegram arrived in Connecticut. Relieved by the assurances and confidence of Marcus and Roger, I had been lulled into a satisfying complacency that all was well. Monica would recover soon, we'd all wanted to believe. Monica always got well. "Why didn't Roger tell me?"

"He doesn't know. No one but you does, Allison. And you mustn't tell them."

"But why? Surely you should be resting, there must be something, some treatment." I was crying.

"Oh, do shut up, Allison. Always overemotional, and you talk about me being dramatic. No wonder you went to America and stayed there.

"I don't want to be fussed over, don't want to feel that overwhelming, enervating pity. I don't want to be coddled, I want to live as much as I can while I can. Promise me you won't say anything to any one, not even Roger. He couldn't bear knowing."

Why me then, *why me?* I wanted to scream at her. Why not Roger—he was her husband. How would I, even as her closest sister, bear the knowledge? How could I keep quiet, let Monica carry on as usual? How would I carry on as usual? The horror of it all dragged me into anger as Monica continued talking, telling me that she was the one who needed strength, what I needed was some backbone.

I jumped up and held her. For a moment she allowed it then gently pushed me away saying, in a quiet, loving voice, "That's it, Allison, no more spontaneous emotional hugs and sighs. You make it worse. I'm alive *now*." She looked at me intently. "This summer is important for me. There are things to do before I die, and I need this time to arrange them." She stood up to get more coffee. "I'm not entirely resigned to it myself, but it helps to have told you. I needed to do that. But I'm not an invalid yet, don't treat me like one."

"All right, Monica. I'll be the younger sister and follow

your lead, be strong." I said it sadly, feeling as I did so that there was more than a little bitterness in my statement.

Monica, dear Monica, had taken the loads of all of us, been mother, father and guiding light. She was so positive about everything too. Surely there must have been times when she hadn't wanted younger siblings, the responsibility of the family and its finances, of maintaining all of us; an emotional prop for Roger and Snowsdown too. Her success in keeping it all together indicated that she must have thrived on it. Monica liked power, not just family power but professional and public power, and she had all three: She was an impeccable scholar with a degree in classics and an advanced degree in archeology from Cambridge, dozens of articles and three books on the Bronze Age to her credit. And then, with the advent of television in the early fifties, a whole new career as a personality discussing subjects ranging from local myths of witch murders to strange markings on Etruscan or Phoenician pots. And finally, her own series on Ancient Greece, which had even been shown in America.

Monica, who hadn't known her own mother, remembered ours, and then, with the birth of Marcus, our mother's death. We only knew her from photographs, stories told by Father and Monica, and a large portrait which hung in the study. A woman they say I resemble in a startling way. Our father, lost and incomplete without her, had lived thirty aimless years leaving all decisions and problems to Monica. She had cared for us and perhaps controlled too much. With Father's death ten years ago she had inherited everything officially in trust—the house, estates, money—and the reins tightened. I was the one who'd gone away long ago. Willow had married Clive but was still dependent, and Marcus had stayed to run the orchards and farms. I thought they were perhaps not as nostalgic as I for the times before, that the yesterdays of a lifetime with Monica had been more than they'd wanted.

"Let's not talk of it any more," she said now. "Let's talk about life. Where's that daughter of yours, I haven't met her yet. Last time she was here she was three months old, and not wearing blue denim."

I rose and went to call her from the lawn. She was no longer standing on it, but spread-eagled, face burrowing into the lushness of it.

"Just getting the smell of it all," she said, lifting her face. "I'm going to like it here, Mother. Can we take that walk now? I've been waiting for you."

I took her to meet Monica who was waiting impatiently for us in the drawing room. She didn't hear us enter and her face in repose looked sad. Monica wasn't, had never been, an immediately beautiful woman. To be seen properly, she had to be watched with people. She blossomed as a million expressions roamed her face when she talked or listened; the way she walked or sat, the movement of her hands, gave an intensity that made her beautiful in motion. She turned and as her glance fell on Jennifer, her face lost its quiet sadness. It burst into a dozen lines of laughter and interest, lines that could never age her.

"My dear, it's good to see you again, you've changed." She laughed and held out her hand to Jennifer who took it. She was about to shake hands but changed her mind as she looked at her aunt; she leaned forward to kiss her.

"Just like your mother, I see. Do all Americans kiss each other so much?" she asked.

Jennifer, not given to emotional displays either, pulled back embarrassed and startled. "I don't know," she said. "I'm just glad to see you Aunt Monica."

Monica was pleased and pulled Jennifer on the couch beside her. They looked so different, one gray and old, the other dark, life bursting through every pore. And yet, like conspirators, their bodies leaning against one another, they looked very much alike as each took the measure of the other. Jennifer had to weigh the reality with the legend. I'd told so many stories, boasted about Monica for so many years. I hoped I hadn't raised too many expectations in Jennifer's mind. I wanted her to love Monica as we all did, to be infuriated, angry and charmed by her. I looked at them and had few worries. Monica was asking Jennifer about school, pleased to hear that she might go on to graduate school, that she'd been accepted in the graduate program at Harvard. Jennifer hadn't decided whether she really did want to become an anthropologist, and Monica reassured her. It was summer, there was time to make decisions.

There was a commotion of doors slamming and noise from the hall and Marcus stormed into the room. "Has anyone seen Colin?" he asked. "There's going to be a frost and we're short-handed. I need him to work with the men in setting the lanterns."

He left quickly, shouting into the house for Colin, who came running across the lawn as Marcus moved outside. They stood talking for a moment and came back together.

A frost could be disastrous, the fruit killed overnight. The lanterns would be placed beneath the rows of fruit-bearing trees on which Snowsdown depended heavily for its livelihood. The small heat generated by the fires from the lanterns was enough to save the fruit from destruction. It was also a beautiful sight, to stand in the cold, clean night air and watch acres of lights flickering through the shadows of the trees.

Colin *was* handsome, filled into the promise of the man I'd seen in a small boy ten years ago. His hair was very fair and he was tall, his skin young and tanned. He greeted me shyly and shook my hand. A nephew who vaguely remembers his American aunt but knows her as a definite part of his family. "I've met Jennifer," he said, then grinned at her.

He turned, "What time's lunch, Mother?" he asked Monica. "If we've got to get the lanterns out we have to move quickly."

"It's a cold one," she said, "and you'll have to fix your own. Mrs. Potter and her daughter will be back tomorrow." She turned to me, "They're off at her sister-in-law's funeral in Upper Pershing today." Willow, it seemed, would be in charge of dinner. She came in then, bustling and anxious to assure Monica that everything was under control. She was followed by her daughter. Caroline was stunning. A tall girl, a fine complexion, high cheeks in a heart-shaped face centered in smooth, shoulder-length, golden hair. Her riding clothes—britches and hacking jacket—were perfectly and expensively cut. She was a shock. You don't expect to see *Vogue* in your own drawing room. No wonder she and Jennifer hadn't reacted to each other favorably—their styles and probably their temperaments were very different.

Willow was fussing, plumping Monica's pillows, asking Caroline if she was warm enough.

"Oh, Mother, stop it," Caroline snapped, moving away from Willow's concern. She was an anxious, impatient girl, and it was easy to see why Jennifer had been upset. But the veneer might not be too thick; it might be a facade for shyness. We were introduced by Willow, but Caroline turned away quickly, interrupting Colin's conversation with Marcus.

"I thought we were riding again this afternoon, Colin. You can't spend all day with those lanterns," she said.

"You'll just have to go by yourself," said Colin. "Perhaps Jennifer will go with you." He turned to ask her if she rode, but before Jennifer could answer, Caroline had stalked out of the room.

Monica covered Caroline's rebuff by suggesting that Jennifer and I take a walk with her. "Let's go out to the Folly," she said turning to me. "I'd like you to see what I've been up to out there."

We stepped out to the lawns and their borders of daffodils. The gardens hadn't changed: the greenness, the gold of the flowers stretched before us. In the far corner the rock garden with its blue and white flowers running wildly over the varied rocks looked as it always had. On the other side of our path was Roger's rose garden, with blooms climbing the elaborate trellis he'd erected. Even the single willow tree was still leaning toward the small pond beneath it. It was all there, the garden I'd hardly noticed and hadn't liked at all when I was growing up. I could never recognize and name the flowers and plants and suddenly remembered Roger's fatherlike impatience with my inability to learn them. The more he pressured the more I'd resisted. Now, with rebellion over the garden many years behind me, I could relish its lushness. It wasn't important that I didn't know a sweetpea when I saw one.

Monica and Jennifer walked ahead, Monica explaining the house, the maze and its Folly. It was an old house, built between 1600 and 1605 by Sir Bradford Pershing. It had been a distinguished family for several centuries, its reputation built upon the first Sir Bradford's pirating adventures with Raleigh. Royal favor can last a long time, but it could also, in those days, disappear overnight. Sir Bradford's great, great grandson, Sir Poynton Pershing, had lost it. A Puritan who'd fought for Cromwell, he had begun the long road to poverty for the Pershings. With the return of King Charles and the death in battle of Sir Poynton, the family had foundered. It was a long, slow curse but in 1800 the last Sir Bradford Pershing committed suicide and his wife, slightly mad, sold Snowsdown Manor for "a pittance" to my ancestor, the robust merchant, Walter Sherbourne. A romantic history until then.

Walter Sherbourne was born to be a merchant, he prospered in silks and spices in London and sank his money into the land surrounding the Manor. The richest countryside in all of England, it responded to care with an abundance of orchards and farmlands. We were middle-class gentry by now, untitled but rather wealthy. At least Monica was.

"As Hampton Court Maze is modeled upon Versailles, so the maze of Snowsdown is modeled upon Hampton Court," she lectured to a rapt Jennifer. "It's one of the few remaining in England." She expanded on her pet theme.

"Odd in a way. The English like the formality of controlled gardens, and the maze is a perfect example of the English mind. A labyrinth of complexity but a way in and a way out, a solution. We English like puzzles with solutions." She laughed and Jennifer with her. I chuckled at Monica's pomposity, she turned and in her eyes agreed with me.

"Walter Sherbourne built this," I told Jennifer. "A plain man with pretensions."

"No, not quite that," Monica disagreed. "An eccentric—another English phenomenon. The Dutch developed Escher, the French, Sartre, the Americans their Constitution and the English their eccentrics. We don't merely tolerate them, we cultivate them. They have no obvious purpose, just like follies, but they are important to our sense of the ridiculous. Can you imagine Sartre building a folly?"

We were in the maze now, its ten-feet-high privet hedges cutting out the way. It was a dark green, silent, enveloping world. There was no sound from the birds or anything from the outside world, just the tread of our feet on the leaves and small branches beneath them. I didn't remember the way; the code was gone from my mind. We followed Monica blindly.

"Go left on entering," she explained. "Then on the first two occasions when there is an option, go right, but then thereafter go left. Remember the pattern and you'll always find the center of the maze, not only here but at Hampton Court and Versailles too," she told us.

"I imagine it feels like this to fly a glider or dive deep beneath the sea," said Jennifer in reverent tones. "It's eerie.

We're in a world of our own, depending on different senses. And lovely."

She was right, for the moment. Then it opened and the hedges receded. We had reached the center of the maze, a patch of open land. Sitting squarely upon it was Walter Sherbourne's Folly—a miniature, but sizable replica of the Parthenon, square with columns, open to any sun and breeze that might find its way into the maze of tall privet. I could see what Monica had been doing. The Folly was gleaming white, recently painted, the broken columns rebuilt, the crumbling plaster patched and covered with clever work. We climbed the step to its base and I saw that Monica had brought chairs and tables into its room, white wrought-iron chairs of classical design with modern glass-topped wrought-iron tables. There were plants everywhere, tall ones on the floor, small ones under the glass of the tables, more hanging from above; evergreens that would survive without too much light. In an odd way, with strange formality and ease, it all worked. Monica sat down and everything fell into place. It was a setting for people, and Monica made it real. Jennifer and I sat with her.

"Why have you been renovating this place, Monica?" I asked. It had been years since it had been important to any of us. The children were all grown and I couldn't imagine that any of them had either the time or interest to come out here now. It seemed pointless, and I said as much to Monica, who laughed.

"A folly isn't built for practical reasons, so why should it be used for them?" The flowing lines of her clothes were caught in the breeze, her hand in gesture of waving away my question; a large hat flopped around her face and it was difficult to see her expression, but her voice was momentarily low as if coming from a distance. "I have a whim," she said. "Remember the times we had here, the picnics and later the parties? We were very gay then, all living at home, lots of people always staying over. The maze and Folly added a special excitement to it all." Her voice livened again, came rollicking back to say she wanted a good old-fashioned family picnic. "But Monica," I said incredulously, "renovating the Folly surely isn't necessary for that. Why this place has been crumbling as long as I can remember."

"That's beside the point." She stood up, opening her arms as if to embrace the past. "I have a whim, it's as simple as that. I want to have an elaborate picnic, just as we used to when Father was alive. And besides," she gleamed in a way that brooked no discussion, "I'm an invalid now and should be indulged."

Jennifer jumped up in her endearing but ungainly fashion, laughing at Monica's antics. "So what's all the fuss about a picnic?"

"No fuss, my dear, no fuss," called Monica as she stalked off toward an exit path. "But a picnic at Snowsdown is an event." She disappeared, leaving Jennifer and me to follow at our own pace.

"What does she mean, Mother? Why is a picnic such a big *event* around here?"

"It's not just an event, darling," I explained, "not just cucumber sandwiches or fried chicken. It's a production. The picnic your Aunt Monica's thinking about involves an elaborate, traditional treasure hunt."

Jennifer was puzzled. I smiled at her obvious confusion.

"Come on," I said, urging her along, explaining as we went. "The clues are given in a series of doggerel verses. They've been known to take days to unravel."

"But what's the treasure?" she asked. "It'd better be worth spending all that time hunting for."

"I don't know. It's obviously going to be Monica's picnic. And why the Folly? Ask her."

A treasure hunt was a strange whim of Monica's. We hadn't had one since Father's death. He was the poet, the romantic who'd always written the clues, hidden the treasure and conducted the events and discovery with glee. Monica, it seemed, was planning a revival.

CHAPTER 3

The family gathered together in the library after dinner. It was an old and comfortable tradition. Monica was ensconced in the brocade, straight-backed chair; the centerpiece of the lofty room. The bookcases on three walls were in shadow, but their presence lent an aura of warmth to the proceedings. The fourth wall was lined with french doors, now closed and hidden by velvet drapes against the night. The lighting was subdued, and I caught expressions only when someone stood before the fire or leaned toward Monica. She was holding court, excited by having the family together again. Roger was offering brandy, Willow fluttering behind Monica's chair. Colin and Jennifer were lounging on the sofa and Marcus was talking to Caroline about the lanterns they'd set for the night's frost. She looked bored. The family, together again. But things had changed and I saw the passage of time as Jennifer moved across the room toward Monica. She was wearing a long peasant dress. With hair up and a glow from the fire on her face she gave the impression of having stepped from the past century rather than across the room. Monica caught her hand as Jennifer leaned to speak to her, but before any words were exchanged the tall double doors from the hallway opened and Monica's glance moved beyond Jennifer to smile at Carrington who entered the room. He was followed by Eleanor and a young man I gathered must be his nephew, Nicholas.

"Carey, darling, we've been waiting for you. I want you to meet my niece," Monica cried.

He moved easily and, in spite of his age, with a young man's stride toward Jennifer. He took her hand and brought it to his lips. "I am delighted to meet you, my dear. Especially as I can see in Monica's eyes the joy you're bringing to her."

Jennifer was at a loss with such old-world charm, and I fancy she almost curtsied. Carrington had always had that effect on me too. He was, I felt, one of the few romantic visions in the world, the rare man who could wear his white handkerchief elegantly tucked in the sleeve of his jacket. He used it effectively, bringing to mind an age when all men wore ruffled shirts and bloused sleeves. He kissed Monica's cheek and turned to greet the room.

"Allison," he beamed and came toward me arms outstretched. "You are lovelier than ever." He grasped my shoulders and brushed my cheek with his, "We've missed you my dear, very much."

Haughty, elegant Eleanor was right behind her father. "Hello, Allison." I smiled politely, tightly, my face already beginning to feel the strain, and felt as if a cold breeze swirled around my shoulders. We had never particularly cared for each other, she had always seemed removed from any emotions. I wondered now, as I had in the past, about her love for Marcus. Did he not notice how cold she was? But perhaps she did love him, showed him a tenderness that I hadn't seen in many years. She had been friendly when we were children and suddenly, it seemed, she didn't need us any more. "This is cousin Nicholas," she continued, bringing forward the tall young man with glowing dark hair. If he hadn't been looking so taciturn he would have been extremely attractive. He nodded in my direction and moved away toward Roger and the brandy. But Monica caught him first. "Nicholas, stop being so miserable and come here to meet my niece." As Jennifer and Nicholas looked at each other, I could see the interest in his eyes. Suddenly he smiled and became an attractive young man. "Forgive me." He turned and smiled at me too. "I lost one of Shea's pups in the river this afternoon."

He looked a bit defiant as he admitted the source of his misery, and suddenly I could see his resemblance to Carrington's dead wife, Jessica. She had been the loveliest woman in the county, so they say, when she was young. She was pursued and courted by young men from all over England, but it was Carrington, a neighbor's son, who caught her eye. They married and bought the property next to Snowsdown. After a while Jessica was pregnant with Eleanor; the baby was born and Jessica contracted polio. She was confined to her bed for the next ten years and until her death she wore that defiant, proud look I'd just seen fleetingly on Nicholas' face. He was Jessica's sister's son.

Amidst the swirlings and greetings, Caroline's voice suddenly pierced the warm conversation. "Do you all know, Jennifer thinks we have ghosts?" Her tempered voice was mocking, shattering the pleasure I had felt in being home. "Do you know, she saw a gray figure in her room last night? Perhaps it was poor, suicidal Lady Poynton."

All attention was directed at Caroline. All movement, all

conversation had stopped, everyone was caught in a tableau of consternation. I looked across at Jennifer, still leaning toward Colin, listening to something he was saying to her. Stunned and confused, she turned toward Caroline.

"Would you believe, ghosts at Snowsdown? Why, not even Lady Poynton warrants a ghost, and that's the most exciting thing that's ever happened here," Caroline continued. She was becoming annoyed, the room was quiet, no one was laughing. She tossed her head and strained to rouse some laughter. "You all know it's ridiculous. Why it's *funny* Jennifer should imagine such a thing."

Colin smiled vaguely and said, "Oh, come off it, Caroline."

She turned on him, flaring, "You thought it amusing enough this morning, my dear. You laughed quite loudly, as I recall." He blushed and turned away.

Jennifer had moved toward Caroline, but before she could speak Monica stood, took her hand and turned toward Caroline. "You've never had an imagination, Caroline." Slim and elegant, laughter in her voice, she turned to Jennifer, "I'm glad someone in the family has. There's nothing worse than lack of imagination and no sense of humor."

The tension eased as we all laughed with Monica and picked up our interrupted conversations. Caroline, furious, turned and pushed her mother aside, "Oh, stop it, Mother, stop hovering."

Willow was crying. Ineffectually Clive tried to make his daughter apologize. Ignoring him Caroline grabbed Colin and took him to a corner of the room where they engaged in angry conversation.

Sherbourne's Folly

It had all happened so quickly. Dinner had been fun, we'd all helped Willow in the kitchen before going off to our rooms to dress in our party clothes for this first family reunion in years. We had laughed and remembered old times. Monica was in good form. We all were. Bubbling with affection, and not a little wine, we had moved into the library for coffee and brandy, to await the arrival of Carrington and Eleanor. But Caroline: It was clear that we weren't all happy and full of affection, of love for each other.

I moved toward Jennifer; it had all happened so quickly and she was still stunned by Caroline's mocking dislike. "It's all right, Mother," she said as I approached her. "I think Caroline is mad at me because I seemed to be getting so much attention from everyone." She was right, of course, but even an image from *Vogue* had no excuse to be so unkind.

"What is the matter with that girl, Monica?" I asked quietly. Monica dismissed her, "I don't know, she's been selfish and impossible ever since she returned from that French finishing school Willow sent her to." Monica seemed flustered and vague, almost uncomfortable. "Let's not talk about it any more. Caroline's being characteristic." She sat down, once more the center of our gathering. Holding Jennifer's hand she turned to Carrington, the three of them joining together in dismissing Caroline and the scene she'd caused.

It wasn't so easy for me. Or Willow. Poor, distracted Willow, frightened and anxious and nervously picking up empty coffee cups, moving them to the sideboard.

"Now that everyone's here, Aunt Monica, tell us about

the picnic and treasure hunt," Jennifer asked. "You've kept me waiting all day." Relief spread through the room and we gathered around. "Come on, old girl," said Roger. "You've kept the young ones in suspense long enough. Your stage is set." We all smiled as Roger enjoyed Monica's dramatics. "The rest of us would like to know your schemes too."

On stage, enthroned, Monica posed with deliberation, crossing her legs and allowing the fabric of her skirts to mold their elegance with kindness and style. She lit a cigarette which she then placed in a slim, black holder. All very studied and all so perfect.

Remembering and enjoying Monica's preparations, I looked around this room. So many hours and years spent here. I loved it and I loved these people. Roger in his distinguished way was leaning casually against the back of Monica's chair, a man totally at ease with himself and yet still surprised that Monica, so rare a creature, was his wife. Carrington, his sweet, lined and lean face caught in the light from the fire moved to sit on the couch with Jennifer who looked flushed, excited and a bit unsure of herself, still trying to pull herself together from Caroline's attack. Colin had come from the corner where he'd talked with Caroline and sat at my daughter's feet. He whispered something to her, she smiled briefly, shrugged and leaned back. Nicholas, darkly handsome, sat on the back of the couch, one leg idly swinging, a cigarette in his right hand. Eleanor and Marcus, both straight and tall and fair, stood with drinks in hand leaning against a bookcase. It was hard to see their expressions, but my feeling was one of some discord. Willow and Clive looked even less comfortable as they moved to chairs, to become part of the group; a little forlorn as their daughter continued to glower from the back of the room.

"Come and sit here, Mother," called Jennifer. Carrington made room and I sat beside him. He took my nervous hand in his cool one and held it loosely as Monica prepared her moment.

"There's not much to tell, my darlings," she said from center stage. In this moment Monica's charisma engaged us all. Easy to understand her fame and success. "I want to have one of those grand old-style parties we used to have when Father was alive. At my age I can be allowed to think there was something magic about those days, that summers were better, days longer and all the other clichés old people say about the old days all the time." She paused for a moment, allowing us to understand that she was not wallowing in nostalgia but rather mocking it.

I heard a sigh from Eleanor and then from Marcus, "Do get on with it, Monica," impatience in his voice.

"Oh, Marcus," I said, "you know Monica's going to do it her way. Just relax and listen."

As if there'd been no interruption, Monica sailed along. It was curious listening to her. She had experienced the parties, the treasure hunts, as a young woman. I had been just a child. Hearing Monica's version made me suddenly yearn for John, alone in Connecticut. John, a lawyer, used to do court work, and sometimes I would go and listen to his cases. There could be ten witnesses to any one incident, and even allowing for ten different perceptions, there could be ten true versions of an event. I was struck with sudden pangs of loneliness, but I forced myself to listen to Monica saying that traditions shouldn't be allowed to lapse—they brought us together.

It was going to be very simple. Monica was going to write several verses, each a clue. We were going to track them down and the winner would find the treasure. "I want to give you all something," she said. "I promise the treasure is important in different ways to each of you."

With this enigmatic statement she rose. "I'm very tired —I'm going to bed. Will you help me, Jennifer?" She stood awkwardly, her elegance subdued by weariness.

It is curious how time is an accumulation of events and moments that kaleidoscope into the immediate. Monica accuses me of being overly sentimental about things past. Perhaps she's right, but as I too age, I think it's less sentimentality than a striving to gain some perspective about where I am now and where I have been.

Memory is stirred by many things. Being back at Snowsdown, fitting so easily into old patterns, old antagonisms, old alliances and loves, my memory was sharpened. For twenty years I had been away from all this, and yet it had gone on, the changes in people, in me, too subtle to grasp immediately.

Carey must have been thinking in much the same way. As Monica swept off to her room he suggested a walk in the gardens, a breath of fresh air. "You'll need a warm wrap, my dear, there is a slight frost." He held his arm for mine and we left the glow of the library for the stark clearness of the night. It was a night of brilliance, the northern stars overwhelming with their density. Our breath hung in the air as we sauntered slowly through the freshly budding trees and plants that for the moment held the scent of promises to come. We were quiet and comfortable together, and I felt a surge of joy at the peace I felt all around, with Carey, with me.

I broke the silence with my thoughts. "Carey, I'm filled with so many memories."

"So am I, my dear, so am I. Seeing you after all these years, truly more beautiful than ever, the young girl blossomed. I am filled with pleasure and a little sadness about all of us, about time."

"Why sadness, Carey?"

His voice was quiet but alive, and for the moment, in spite of the pressure of his arm, I felt him far away. "Sadness for the alternatives we'll never know. Tonight looking at all of you, my mind wandered to moments passed, moments not grasped. I've been thinking of Jessica, of how her illness, her death, changed my life and perhaps even more profoundly changed Eleanor's life."

We continued walking aimlessly along the paths of the garden. For a moment Carey was quiet and I didn't interrupt his thoughts. I did want him to continue, wanted to know how he felt about Eleanor and Marcus, whether he had any inkling that Monica wasn't as well as she pretended.

"I feel that my daughter's life is passing her by." He turned to me, "And I feel Marcus' life passing by too. Eleanor was a good-hearted, bright child, she was alive and loving. Then Jessica died and gradually she withdrew from me, from everyone. When she fell in love with Marcus I thought everything would be good for her again. But the engagement goes on and on, they don't talk about marriage, they don't do anything, go anywhere. There's no joy, and it makes me very sad."

"Why don't they marry? What are they waiting for?" I asked.

"I'm afraid they're waiting for security. They want guarantees, and they see that in terms of land—this land," he spread his arms to embrace the gardens, the orchards and farmlands beyond.

I was angry. "What you're saying, Carey, is that they're waiting for Monica to die." He didn't acknowledge what I'd said except in the tightening of his lips, the quickening of our pace. "They don't need Monica's money and land. Marcus is secure here. There wouldn't be a farm and orchards without him."

Carey's voice was strangled as he said in reply, "Eleanor wants it. She's determined to be lady of the manor, and Marcus is too lily-livered to tell her that she's unreasonable. And I think he does love her, and what she wants has become what he wants."

I had never seen Carey so tortured before, never imagined that he could say these things about his own daughter, and I felt indignant that he could.

His smile was sad, "I know what you're thinking, Allison, but I've lived with Eleanor all of her life. I know her. I've tried talking with her, tried to show my love for her, to take care of her. These are not easy things to acknowledge, far less easy to say."

All I could do was kiss his lined, elegant cheek, take his arm again and move us forward into our walk. I was shocked by his outburst, but as we turned and walked back toward Snowsdown, toward the lights of the house competing, and failing dismally, with the stars, I had to think he was probably right. I had thought so many ungenerous thoughts about Eleanor myself. I'd seen her bitterness, her control over Marcus.

He brought me back from my wandering thoughts with a tightening of his hand on my arm. "I did say pleasure as well as sadness," he smiled gently. "Monica. She is joy and beauty. It seems that I have always adored her. I've known her all my life, and other than Greece, always at Snowsdown."

Tonight was full of surprises. "In Greece? You went to Greece together?"

He was off in his own world again and I, wanting to hear more, let it ride until he was ready to tell me. "No, we didn't go together. Monica was on a dig and I had to go for that export company I used to work for. We met, as friends do, in a strange city and Monica showed me her Greece, and we discovered a new one together." He looked at the night sky. "The sky in Greece is different, by day and by night. It's golden even when dark, the moon casts different shadows, throws a different light. The sounds and stillness are different. It's a quality I can still feel two decades later."

He stopped suddenly. "It was all a long time ago. Monica went back to her dig and I came home. When she returned to England she married Roger."

We were back at the house and Carey didn't want to talk any more. I wondered whether they'd had an affair, but it seemed too late to ask. "I won't come in with you, Allison, it's late. I talk too much and I'm very tired." He pulled me to him and for a moment I rested my head on his shoulder. We parted and I went back into the house full of Carey and his revelations.

Exhausted by my first day at home, my intention had been to go immediately to bed. Obviously some alcohol had been consumed by the remaining members of our group, and I heard voices raised in shrill anger as I walked past the library door. I would have passed by if I hadn't heard Eleanor's voice raised and directed at my daughter.

Although I was tired, Carey's thoughts about Eleanor compelled me back to the library. I wanted to try and *see* her, wanted to believe that she was not as bitter and anxious and grasping as Carey thought. It was one thing for me not to care for her; it was another to believe anything really bad about her. The fire in the library had died down but Eleanor and Marcus, Jennifer and the two boys were still there. They stopped talking and watched me cross the room. It looked peaceful enough, but there was tension in the air which made it difficult for me to feel comfortable as I walked to join the group.

Jennifer smiled and made room for me beside her on the couch as Eleanor said, "And how was Daddy, Allison? I have a feeling he bored you with family stories." Her voice was questioning and a little bitter.

"No, I wasn't bored. We did talk about the family, even about Greece, but mostly we walked and enjoyed being with each other again."

Eleanor was an attractive woman. Physically she reminded me of a tall, lean, streaked-blonde socialite I'd once met from Houston. Not an English look at all. Until she spoke, when the clear tones of her voice, her gestures, dimmed that particular American look. If you didn't know she was thirty-five it would be hard to guess her age. She would probably look as good in ten or twenty years as she did now. At first glance she seemed a woman at ease with herself, but an occasional pursing of her mouth, an anxious look to her eyes belied that. She was highly strung and in tight control. I had never seen Eleanor lose her temper, but I could feel a rage inside her which let loose wouldn't be very pleasant.

"Greece," she said now. "That's something he never mentions to me. He and Monica were there at the same time, weren't they?"

I nodded and, not wanting to discuss it with Eleanor, said rather curtly that Monica had been on a dig and Carey there on business. She looked at me a little oddly, almost as if she wanted to ask a question, but she didn't pursue it.

Whatever had been going on before I walked into the room was obviously not going to be picked up again. I had a feeling that my appearance and refocusing of the conversation was welcome. The atmosphere had relaxed slightly, but there was still a feeling around me of voices pitched in anger and irritation. I was feeling rather battered by new—to me—problems of the family and by Monica's approaching death. I was glad to be excluded from whatever had happened while I was out walking with Carey. I stood, admonished Jennifer not to stay up too late, and went to the comfort of my room.

CHAPTER 4

I had hardly settled in bed with the nineteenth century when Jennifer burst into my room. I was forced to put Trollope aside and give her my undivided attention.

"Forgive me, Mother," she said, "but there's so much bad feeling around. I don't understand it. Why is Caroline so vicious to me, and what do you think Colin and Eleanor are up to?"

"Caroline's vicious, as you put it, because she feels left out and uncomfortable, I imagine. But what do you mean about Eleanor and Colin?"

Jennifer was flushed and upset, with her hair and clothes awry. Caught up in my own memories and emotions, it suddenly seemed that I had not been paying enough attention to Jennifer's problems in confronting her English family for the first time. I moved my feet aside and held out my hand and she came to sprawl across the bottom of my bed.

"Well, you know, Mother, they were huddled together for ages after you and Carrington left. It seemed very intense, and Colin was upset. It seemed to me that Eleanor was telling Colin something he didn't want to hear."

"It could have been anything, darling. We've just arrived and have very little idea of what goes on around here.

All we see are the feelings, hostilities as well as love, built up over years of being with each other."

She agreed but thought that there had been something particularly unpleasant and furtive about that conversation. "They were on the terrace, and when Caroline turned the lights on out there they moved off. Eleanor came back into the library, but it was ages before Colin joined us. He was very subdued.

Until now I'd dismissed the raised voices I'd heard. "What was Eleanor so angry about? I heard her when I came back from walking with Carey."

Jennifer looked puzzled. "I don't really know. She was just ranting about American relatives coming over and thinking they know everything. She assured me that I didn't, and that my dear Aunt Monica shouldn't be taken too seriously—that she was just flattering me while it was convenient."

As I listened to Jennifer, I realized how very removed I really was from Snowsdown and everything that went on here. My feelings were old feelings, our relationships hadn't grown or changed in twenty years. It was, in a curious way, more difficult than staying with strangers because then I wouldn't have imagined that I did know anything about them. I'd arrived at Snowsdown thinking I knew where everything was, who we were. It had been a rather short-sighted and short-lived belief.

Jennifer made motions to leave. "I guess I'm just a bit too anxious for it all to work. I want your family to like me." She leaned over to kiss my cheek. "Sleep well, Mother," and was gone.

I gave up entirely on Trollope and gave in to thoughts of my family and turned out the light.

I woke to the sound of a scream in the night. Not an owl or a nightmare, but a scream, piercing my dreams, flinging me from bed and into the blackness of the landing. Doors opening, people calling out, muffled voices in the dark. A scream, a heavy silence, a moan and now the confusion of disturbed bodies, responding to something that is frightening them.

"Lights, dammit, somebody turn on the lights," came Roger's strong voice. The landing and stairs were suddenly ablaze, lights casting shadows along the hallway below. I could see Willow's head looking up at us with blank eyes from the shadows, her hand on the switch to her left. "It's Monica," she said. I looked at her feet and saw that it was Monica. Monica in shadow, vague without light, crumpled and forlorn, a Monica I had never seen, never imagined before. With Willow I stared fascinated as Roger and Marcus pushed me aside as they raced down the stairs.

"She fell," moaned Willow.

Monica stirred, tried to say something, to sit up. I rushed down to her side, pushing Willow away. "What is it Monica, what did you say?" Her words were mumbled, indistinct. I helped her to sit up, leaned closer to hear what she wanted to say.

"Didn't fall. Pushed." She tried to move and I felt her muscles, with some power, stiffening, coming together under my hands. She freed her arms from my restraint and looked up from the floor to the others surging around. "Pushed," she said clearly, distinctly to us all. The effort was momentary and stunning. Her body sagged against me, her energy flew, and she became once more unconscious.

Willow, still in something of a daze, having hardly moved since she first turned on the lights, was repeating Monica's words in a hollow voice, "Pushed," she said.

The implication of Monica's accusation had halted our movements and voices, but Willow's vacant words brought us to action. I rested Monica's head gently on the carpet, stood up and looked at Willow. Her eyes were unfocused, she kept mumbling to herself, over and over, "Pushed. Pushed." I slapped her sharply across the right cheek, and her eyes flashed and focused on me. Before she could respond with anger, Roger had stepped in. "Go and call the doctor, Willow," he said firmly. "Tell him Monica fell down the stairs." Without a word she turned and went into the drawing room to make the call.

"Shall we move her?" Marcus asked, his voice quiet and frightened. "No," said Roger. "Jennifer," he turned to my daughter who was standing quietly at the top of the stairs watching. "Go and fetch a blanket and pillow right away." She moved into her room and in a minute was back and running down the stairs. I took the blanket from her and covered Monica. Roger took the pillow and gently lifted her head, placing it on the pillow.

There was nothing to do until Wyndham arrived. Willow was back, and we all hovered around Monica quietly, not looking at each other. No one sat down. When Marcus tried to ask what Monica had meant about being pushed he was silenced by Roger who had taken charge and at that moment was controlling all of us. "We'll talk to Monica about it later."

It was cold waiting in the dim hall and Clive, who had been a silent witness, went and fetched coats and sweaters for us. As he returned Wyndham arrived, his pajamas, in the traditional way of doctors on night calls, showing beneath his trouser legs. He moved quickly to Monica.

"She seems all right, nothing broken, just concussion and shock. I only hope it wasn't another heart attack. Roger, come here and let's carry her upstairs." Roger lifted her in his arms, a strong man in spite of his age, and together they went to Monica's room.

"Let's have some brandy before we go back to bed," offered Clive. "I've revived the fire in the library, it should be warmer in there."

Marcus was white and shaking, and as soon as brandy was served by Clive he asked again, "What did Monica mean? Why would anyone push her downstairs?"

"Well, certainly not one of us," said Clive, "and there's no one else around. She probably got confused in the dark and slipped."

We looked at each other.

"She may have imagined she was pushed," volunteered Jennifer. "I mean, it *was* dark."

"But what was she doing wandering around in the dark?" Colin asked the question that had been in all our minds. "Light switches are easy enough to find wherever you want to go in this house."

"Isn't there a night light on the landing?" I asked.

"Yes there is," said Colin. He turned and left the room. He was back quickly saying that for some reason there wasn't a bulb in the socket and so it had been pitch black when Monica ventured from her room into the hallway.

Willow was flushed, from my slap and the two glasses of brandy she'd already had. "We can ask Mrs. Potter about it," she said. "She may have just forgotten to replace the old bulb with a new one."

It was curious because as much as anyone possibly could, Monica knew this house. She wouldn't need a light to know where doors were, how many steps. But I kept my thoughts to myself. Circumstances were not usual. Monica was dying. I didn't know what the illness was really doing to her body, although she was visibly weaker.

Roger came back, some relief on his face. "Monica's awake," he reported. "Wyndham's leaving and will be back to check her out thoroughly tomorrow. Doesn't seem to be too serious."

"Did she say anything more about being pushed?" asked Willow.

Roger looked at all of us. "No. She didn't want to talk much. I'm going back up now to sit with her. Wyndham's given her a sedative, she should sleep, but I want to be sure she's all right."

While talking he had served himself a brandy, and now he left the room wearily, glass in hand, and went up to Monica. I knew he would sit in a chair beside her bed for the whole night, what little was left of it. Already the grayness of dawn on a dull day was creeping into the room. It was cold, and I was reminded of bomb shelters after the raids of World War II and we were still alive.

It was late when I went down the next morning. The house was quiet except for Mrs. Potter who brought fresh coffee into the dining room and told me where everyone was. Monica in her room, Willow in hers and everyone else about their errands on the land or in the village. Jennifer had gone over to the Cartwright's to ride with Nicholas.

Mrs. Potter already knew about Monica's fall and was anxious to share her thoughts about Monica wandering around in the dark and her anger at Marcus' suggestion this morning that she had failed to replace the light bulb and that it was her fault that Monica fell.

"Just because my sister-in-law died and I was off at the funeral is no reason to think I wasn't doing my job," she sniffed. "I don't like to be accused of not working."

"Marcus wasn't accusing you, Mrs. Potter. He's upset that Monica fell and wants to know how it happened."

"She fell last week too, out in the Folly. That was no light bulb," she said.

Her point was well taken, but I persisted. "No, but this time it was dark, and there was no bulb in the socket."

"The bulbs for that night light are kept in the drawer of the commode at the top of the stairs," she said. "It's on my list of things to check every week. When I looked at it four days ago, it was lit."

"Well, perhaps someone else saw it had gone out and didn't know where the new bulbs were. Don't worry about it, Mrs. Potter," I said rising and moving to the door. "I'd love some more coffee, will you bring it up to Mrs. Dayer-Smith's room for both of us please, Mrs. Potter?"

I hoped Monica felt well enough to see me. I wanted to find out not only how she felt this morning but whether she still thought she'd been pushed. I moved quietly to her door. There was no sound from within, and I tapped gently so that she could ignore the knock if she wanted.

She didn't. "Come in," her voice was strong and I went in, relieved. It was a gray day, but Monica's room was cheerful. There was a coal fire glowing in the hearth and Monica sat beside it wearing a long red dressing gown, a tartan blanket across her knees and a book in her hand.

"You shouldn't be reading now," I said.

"Why not? Sore bones have nothing to do with my eyesight." I moved into the room and sat opposite her. Monica didn't remember much about the events of the night before.

We were quiet for a few moments as Mrs. Potter knocked and brought in a full pot of coffee and two cups. She placed the trolley between us and left. I poured us each a cup of coffee, Monica's rich with cream, mine black.

"Why were you wandering around so late, Monica?" I asked.

She confessed to not sleeping well and thinking of going to the library to see if there was any fire left and perhaps having a drop of brandy.

"Why do you think you were pushed?" My directness startled her.

"Did I say that I had been?" she asked.

I nodded. "How can you know, Monica? It was so dark."

"If you, my dear, had been pushed down a flight of long, dark stairs, you'd remember it too," she said indignantly.

I tried a new tack. "But it was dark, Monica, and perhaps you bumped into something."

"I was pushed. It isn't the area between one's shoulder blades that bumps into anything. I walked out of my room, the door closed behind me and I realized the hall was

Sherbourne's Folly

dark." She looked at me scornfully when I asked why she hadn't gone back to fetch a light of some kind.

"Allison, I've lived in this house practically all my life. A dark hallway doesn't confuse me, it doesn't disorient me. Why should I need a light to get down a flight of stairs I've walked up and down a million times before? I was pushed." She was adamant.

"Why would any one, and it would have to be one of us, want to push you down stairs, Monica?"

She looked pained and sad. "You don't understand reality, Allison, you never have, and you've been away too long. I control the family money, the house, the land. Just because you're married and live very comfortably in America and don't care about any of it, doesn't mean that others don't."

She was right of course, but that was not reason enough for anyone in our family to try and hurt her. She went on, "After last night's episode I'm beginning to think that the fall from the stepladder in the Folly wasn't an accident either." I looked at her in amazement. "Oh, I know Wyndham says I had a mild heart attack, that I probably had another last night. But the stepladder did wobble and I did fall and I *was* pushed last night." I couldn't believe what Monica was actually saying, that she believed someone wanted her out of the way.

"Oh, Allison, don't be a fool. You know the terms of Father's will. I have financial control, and even if I wanted to let go, there's no way. As long as I'm alive I take care of it all and the people in this family. It's my legal responsibility."

"But any of us, if we needed money, would come to you, Monica," I tried to bring reason to the conversation.

"Well, perhaps you would, Allison, perhaps not. What has happened over the years is that I not only control the family money, I control the family."

She was not, of course, saying things that I didn't know. "Well why didn't you try and do something about that—let go?"

"How could I? The will is iron-clad and, for the most part, things have run smoothly enough. It's only been recently that I've felt an urgency about the house, that something is not right and that I am at the center of it."

She leaned back and looked totally weary. I realized that our conversation had exhausted her. "Leave now, Allison, we can talk later. I'm not sure what I shall do." As I left her room I heard the book she had been reading earlier slip from her knees to the floor.

"You know, Mother, there *is* something going on around here." Jennifer and I were walking around the village as I showed off my childhood, talking about the people I'd known, the things we used to do to entertain ourselves. "What on earth do you mean?" I asked, broken from my own reverie.

"Well, I saw the ghost again last night. I don't care what anyone says, there was something in my room, at the foot of my bed. I woke up and there it was, this shadow, then I wasn't sure, and then it was gone."

My daughter does have an imagination but surely not that much, two nights running. "When did it happen, darling? Do you know what time it was?"

"It was just before Aunt Monica fell down the stairs. I was lying there, trying to get it all together when everything started happening. For a moment I was scared—all that noise, the dark, the ghost."

I could imagine. I couldn't, however, believe that Jennifer was seeing ghosts. I thought I'd ask Monica about it later. I tried to reassure Jennifer and reminded her that she wasn't really sure what she'd seen and suggested that we should exchange rooms one night to see if it still happened. I asked her not to tell the rest of the family.

CHAPTER 5

Monica is not a woman given to unfounded fancy. On some level I had to take seriously her conviction that someone in our family was trying to speed her death. It was, however, *her* conviction, and she was a sick woman; I didn't know whether that knowledge of approaching death could distort her perceptions so drastically. There was no one I could talk to. I had promised Monica not to tell anyone else that she had leukemia and talking about what I thought were her fancies would be just as disloyal. But Carey was soothing to be with, so after lunch I changed into walking shoes and set off across the fields to his house. How I wished John was with me. We would walk together, my arm through his, and talk about Monica and my fears about the family. He would listen, and it would all become quite ordinary and understandable.

Who of us would kill Monica? God knows I have felt like killing Monica, but that has been fleeting, violent anger over basically insignificant things. I've felt like killing John, even Jennifer—the people I love more than anything in the world. That was a passionate anger aroused by misunderstandings and frustrations that left me feeling drained and rather silly. But to kill Monica, or anyone, with premeditation, for money or some sense of release or security, seemed impossible to me. For all of us. We all had lived together and had been formed by each other all of our lives.

There was Eleanor, of course, but that was easy, I disliked her. Carey said she wanted to be lady of the manor. Marcus was her key to the grandness she thought she could thrive on. If Marcus had the house, the lands, money, she would be in control of him and everything else. There is a toughness, a calculating litheness about Eleanor, but could she cold-bloodedly kill Monica? I didn't think so.

And Marcus. Would he kill for Eleanor? He had money, and, for all intents and purposes, he made the decisions about the farm and orchards. They were his. If he could kill, it would have to be for Eleanor, to protect her—perhaps, keep her. There would be nothing subtle about his approach. He would, if brought to it, take a gun and shoot his victim.

Ashamed of my thoughts I strode across the land toward the comfort and calm of Carey. It was a sharp, clear, crisp day with a promise of warmth to come in the air, but my enjoyment of it was marred by the melancholy thoughts swirling through my head.

What about Monica's will? I knew that everything would be divided in some way, that the trust would be broken, that there would not be another Monica controlling everything. I suppose Father had thought leaving everything in trust to Monica the wisest thing. She was so much older, she knew how to run the finances, had been almost an equal with him. But perhaps it had given Monica too much control. I'd gone to America, but Willow and

Marcus, in their different ways, had stayed tied to Monica and Snowsdown.

What about Roger? To me, he seemed like a charming but defeated man dependent on Monica. He adored her, always had, but he had spent so many years in her shadow. I realized then that I didn't know anything about his family, who his parents were, whether he had brothers and sisters, what his passions might have been. He'd always been good old Roger, gentle and kind, a shadow in our lives with little real impact. How did he really feel about Monica? Was he always as calm and loving as he appeared, did he ever cry, reach out? Had Monica been there for him?

Willow wouldn't be interested in more money or land. Her life was with Clive in London, her only passion Caroline. And Colin, a young man, what would he need with it all at this point in his life? Could either of them be hiding seething resentments against Monica? It was true that she was not always what everybody wanted her to be, but Willow had stopped trying for attention years ago, had found her own peace with Monica. Colin had been brought up to be independent, to fend for himself at an early age. Monica had always spent time with him during the holidays, doing her research and traveling during the school year. Perhaps that hadn't been enough. But this was all ridiculous. I couldn't imagine any of us resenting or hating Monica enough to kill her, however strong the desire for money or love. It had all been shared by her the best way she knew how.

Carey's house was in sight. It was much smaller than Snowsdown, a stone cottage set in a small garden.

Eleanor's stables were well away from the house and from this approach couldn't be seen. The house sat there, close to the old Evesham Road, looking splendidly welcoming. Carey was delighted to see me.

"Come in, my dear, come in. What a treat to have you just in time for tea." He took my coat and called to his housekeeper. "Two for tea, Mrs. Lively. Lots of crumpets and buttered scones." He lead me into the living room, a cozy place with a fire burning in the grate, the last light of the day creeping through the mullioned windows.

"You look worn out, my dear. You shouldn't have walked over after being up half the night. How is Monica?"

"Tired, but feeling better. As feisty and determined as always." I sank into a soft chair before the fire and held my hands to it. "It was a nasty fall, it knocked her out for a while."

Mrs. Lively rolled in the tea trolley. He poked at the fire and waited for tea to be served and Mrs. Lively's departure before saying anything further. "Eleanor tells me that Colin said Monica thought she'd been pushed down the stairs." He looked at me curiously.

I was in a quandary. "Monica said she *thought* she'd been pushed, but it's all so unclear. It was dark, she's not well, probably had another mild heart attack. Anything could have happened."

"And who would want to push Monica downstairs?" said Carey wryly.

"You almost sound as if you believe she might have been," I said, surprised.

"No, no," he hastened. "It's impossible. It's just that

Monica is not always an easy woman to be with. I've wanted to wring her neck more than once myself."

I was startled by such feeling in his voice. I thought again of their time in Greece together, the tone of his voice and look in his eyes when he'd talked of it last night.

"Were you ever in love with Monica?" I asked him. It came out before I thought. "I'm sorry, forgive me, I have no right to ask."

He saw my embarrassment. "That's all right, Allison. Yes, I was. A long time ago." It was not a conversation to be pursued and I took another crumpet as he poured me a second cup of tea. There was so much more I wanted to know. Was it when they were in Greece, before or after? What had happened, why hadn't they married? Was it when he was married to Jessica?

I also wanted to ask him about Monica's will but felt too awkward now to ask another impertinent question. He, as much as anyone in the family, probably knew something of its terms. He had known our father and been respected by him. He had been Monica's friend for years. Perhaps they'd even been lovers at some time. He suddenly made it easy to ask.

"Monica's recent accidents must have brought the thought of her death to everyone's mind," he was reflective. "It will be so different without her, with the lands and house separated, the money divided. Sherbourne's Folly will not be the heart of the family as it is now."

"I don't see that, Carey, it will all still be in the family, we're all part of it," I fished for more information.

"But she is the force that brings it all together. Colin will own the house, and probably inherit the bulk of the money, especially Monica's own money. Roger will live there with nothing of his own until his death. Marcus and Eleanor will either live there or build their own house somewhere else on the land which Marcus should inherit. Willow will live in London and spend the money she inherits on Caroline. And you, my dear, will be in America."

He'd told me more or less what I'd guessed. Roger probably wouldn't be part of the will, Colin would be the real inheritor, and the rest of us would basically be taken care of through capital.

"I don't think we're all worrying about that now, Carey. It'll work out," I commented.

"Yes, but I'm an old man now, and I hate to see the possibility of it all changing. My life too is tied up with your family's. There are changes and discontents in the air, things I don't understand that disturb me."

For the first time, Carey looked like an old man as he sat casually in the chair opposite mine. His relaxed, sad face was lined and gray. We sat and talked until it was quite dark and Nicholas came back in time for dinner. He drove me back to Snowsdown in time for my own family dinner.

I walked into the drawing room in time to hear Eleanor call Jennifer "a little bastard." They were all there, even Monica ensconced on the couch, her feet up, dressed in a housecoat that looked like an evening gown, a blanket around her knees.

Usually feisty, Jennifer was totally undone by Eleanor's screeching and began to cry. She fled, pushing me aside as she ran through the door. There was a brief silence as Eleanor stood before the fireplace and lit a cigarette.

"How dare you, Eleanor, how dare you," Monica struggled to get up from the couch.

I went to her. "Stay quiet, Monica." I put my hand on her shoulder and she leaned back.

"Just what was all that about, Eleanor?" I asked her quietly.

"You and that brat of yours have been here two days and everything is in chaos. We were fine before you came. Now it's Jennifer this and Jennifer that, she hangs around Monica, she uses my horses to go riding with Colin and you're so nice I could spit. Why don't you just get on back to America and leave us alone!"

She stalked to the door. "Coming, Marcus?" He was spluttering in confusion. "No," he looked around, "I think I'd better stay."

"Suit yourself then." She turned and slammed through the door. A moment later we heard her car roar off down the driveway.

"Will somebody tell me what's going on around here?" I turned to Roger.

"As far as I can tell," he said, "it happened over nothing. We were all sitting here, Monica was talking about the treasure hunt. Colin and Jennifer walked in, they'd been riding this afternoon. Then Jennifer accidentally knocked Eleanor's drink over as she walked by her and Eleanor began her tirade. I don't know what it's all about." He looked confused and hurt and turned toward Monica. "Do you, my dear?"

"Eleanor's unhappy. I don't know why." She sighed and looked resigned and sad. "Why don't you two get married, Marcus?"

Poor Marcus, he looked so pained. "I don't know why, and sometimes, like now, I don't know whether I want to. I can't do anything with Eleanor's temper and discontent. I used to think I could. We can't live here; we can't live with Carey. What can we do?"

Monica responded furiously. "And I suppose you mean you have no money, that I keep it from you." She struggled up from the couch and went toward him. "Why don't you get your own place? There are cottages in the village to rent, you could live here if Eleanor wasn't so set on having her own home." Her final remark was most cutting of all, and as she said it Marcus seemed to shrink. "If you had any guts, if you were a man with any sense, you'd have got out of this a long time ago. I can always find a good manager. This estate would survive without you."

Roger pulled her away. "Monica, that's not only unfair and unkind, it's not true. Marcus has made this place pay in a way it never has. He cares about this land. Come back, my dear, and sit down. You're not well."

Marcus put his drink down and stood up. "If you'll excuse me, I think I will join Eleanor," and he too left the room.

I turned too. "I'll see how Jennifer is. Calling her a bastard was particularly cruel. And I'm sure Eleanor knew exactly what she was doing."

Monica was ashen. "Give her my love, darling," she said to me. "Ask her to come back and join us for dinner, to forgive us all."

Jennifer was trying to read an Agatha Christie in her room. Her face was puffy and pale. "I hate myself for crying in front of them, especially Eleanor," she said, flinging the book aside as I walked in. "I don't understand what is upsetting her and everybody else around here. I wish we'd never come."

"Frankly, so do I, my dear." I hugged her. "Although I am glad to be here for Monica. She sent you her love and asked that you join us for dinner."

She threw her book aside and leaped off her bed. "I never want to see any of them again."

"Come on, darling," I reached for her hand. "Eleanor and Marcus have left. It'll just be the family."

"And Caroline's gone to a party in Evesham," she said, her face brightening. She looked so young and vulnerable, and I suddenly hated my family for paining her so much. "Colin and I had a marvelous time this afternoon," she said. "We did borrow two of Eleanor's horses and we rode all over the place. Did you know that Lower Pershing used to have the highest permanent maypole in England?" I shook my head. "Then it was struck by lightning, and now it has the third highest maypole in England."

We both laughed and I left her to wash her face and prepare for dinner. I was messy too and changed from mud-splattered slacks and walking shoes to a soft skirt and blouse, tied a scarf around my neck, slipped into a pair of pumps and prepared to join the others for a quiet dinner at home.

I was disturbed by Eleanor's comment to Jennifer and I needed to talk to Monica about it. Jennifer was an orphan, who, through Monica's connections, John and I had adopted in England before we'd left for America.

John and I had met when he was a Rhodes scholar at Oxford. Marcus was about to come down, and he'd invited me up for one last party. It was love at first sight. There was no doubt in my mind at the end of that evening that the American guest was the person I wanted to be with. What most struck me about him was *character*, a sense of himself, an openness to ideas and to other people. We spent the evening together with a dozen other people and the next day he called and asked if he could come over to my hotel. We had tea and he asked me to marry him. I said yes.

And then, frightened, I remembered that I couldn't have children. Years ago I'd fallen off a horse, was seriously hurt and in hospital for weeks. I rarely thought about it, it hadn't been important before. I lay awake that night and worried about telling John. I knew I had to.

"I love you," he said as I finished telling him. "Let's get married, and if we want to, we can adopt children."

"Do you mean it?" Please mean it, please, please, I thought as we sat and stared intently at each other across the small table in one of the local bars I'd felt an appropriate place to announce my news.

"Of course I do." He held my hand tightly and I literally gripped his. "We will make wonderful love together, and if we feel like it we'll share it." Suddenly, he looked worried. "But you, my love, how do you feel about not having children?"

"Don't worry, my womanhood isn't threatened. As for no children, well, I've known for years. If it's all right with you, I feel absolutely, incredibly wonderful."

We married the next month and settled down to a final year at Oxford. Monica brought Jennifer to us a few weeks before we sailed for the States and our Connecticut home.

Dinner was a strained affair. Monica was obviously tired, we were all subdued and didn't linger. Before Roger had a chance to urge Monica to bed, I suggested that it was time for her to retire, that she shouldn't even be up, and that I would assist her to bed. We left the others with their brandies beside the fire in the drawing room.

"Come and visit in my room for a while, Monica," I urged. She nodded as I opened the door and sat her in the chair before the hearth.

I sat on the floor, poked at the fire and for a moment was quite content.

"What is going on, Monica?" I finally asked. "No one knows you're as ill as you are, and yet there are all these strange tensions and undercurrents. I'm particularly upset with Eleanor. That was cruel of her."

Monica looked very frail and answered quietly. "We talked about it this morning, Allison. Somebody wants me dead. Someone in the family can't wait for the trust to be released."

"I've thought about it all day, Monica, and I can't believe it. It's a nightmare. There has to be more than money. You'd give it to any of us, wouldn't you?" I looked at her, surprised that I hadn't thought to ask before.

She was irritated by my question. "Of course I would, you fool. If there was any way around it right now I'd let go of everything. It's me one of you wants out of the way. I can't stand that." Her voice broke and a tear slid down her cheek and I remembered the last time I'd seen her cry. "Don't, Allison, please don't." I'd reached out to touch her arm, hold her hand, offer comfort. "God, I'm so weak right now. It's not just the leukemia—that doesn't bother me too much yet. It's not even the falls, but the idea that I'm in the way. That's unbearable."

"What about Jennifer, darling? We've never talked about her parents since you first brought her to us?"

It had been a Friday evening when Monica called. She was passing through Oxford on her way back to Snowsdown from London. Could she drop by for a cup of tea and a sandwich? John and I were delighted. We hadn't seen her for almost a year, just after our wedding. She'd been in Greece on a dig and giving lectures for several months and only recently returned.

Her mission was not only a reunion. She was sad and quiet when she arrived, not the ebullient Monica I was used to. Something was wrong, and I asked her what it was. "Do you remember my old friend Maggie Davis? We were up at Oxford together and she, like you, married an American and went off to live in Texas?" That I didn't remember Maggie Davis wasn't important, Monica continued. "She and Frank were in England this past year. When I returned from Greece I called them in London and discovered they'd both been killed in a car wreck." Monica cried then and told us about their new baby, only two months old, with no immediate family to take care of her. Monica had thought of adopting the child, but with her life-style it didn't seem a good idea for either one of them.

John and I looked at each other. "Why can't we adopt her, Monica?" She made all the arrangements and Jennifer came into our lives.

"She's become a daughter to be proud of, Allison. The last time I saw her she was less than a year old and you were all off to America. It doesn't seem like twenty years to me."

Since we'd been back at Snowsdown I'd felt this growing need to know about Jennifer's parents. At the time of adoption John and I had been so overwhelmed, we'd asked very little of Monica. We'd gone with her to a small town in Somerset called Dunster where Jennifer had been born. The town clerk had presented us with some papers, and we'd gone on to a solicitor to have them all signed and Jennifer was ours. "You know, Jennifer has never asked about her real parents. Of course we told her they were killed just after she was born, but for some reason we never mentioned they were friends of yours," I said, turning to look at Monica.

"It's all so long ago, Allison, it doesn't seem important any more. Why do you worry?"

"It's being back here, I think, feeling some resentment from the family toward Jennifer. I suppose it's the younger people. So much anger bottled up. And they do resent her, you know."

"I think that's true," she said, "but I also think young people are always wary of each other when they first meet. They're not confident enough about themselves yet."

She rose, "I'm very tired, Allison, I need to go to bed." She left and walked slowly from the room. I too felt weary yet continued to sit before the fire watching its embers sink through the grate and splutter into ash.

My reflections didn't last for long. There was a commotion from the landing. I rushed out and saw Monica, energy and fury flowing through her. In spite of her tiredness, her recent tears, our conversation about the past, she looked like the old, vibrant Monica. I began to smile but her words caught me unaware.

"Who the hell has been in my room, going through my things?"

I rushed over to her door and into the room. It looked as it always did to me, everything in its place, neat and orderly. "What do you mean?" I asked, still ready to smile.

"I know somebody's been going through the drawers over there. I know my mattress has been moved, my books disturbed. I know." She swept me aside and ran down the stairs to the drawing room where Roger, Willow and Clive were still sitting.

She launched into the room and everyone jumped up. "What is it, Monica?" Roger rushed to her and placed his arm around her shoulder. She pushed it aside.

"I'm tired of all this. What is going on? Who has been searching through my belongings?" They all looked puzzled.

Willow stood next to Clive, who placed an arm around her and she welcomed it. "Monica, we've been here together all evening. Why would we want to go through your possessions?" she asked.

"I don't know why. Probably looking for my will." Monica, suddenly drained, sat down. "Fix me a brandy, Roger. I was pushed down stairs last night, my room has been searched tonight. Somebody wants me dead."

We all protested loudly, angry. Willow began to cry. "Where are Marcus and Eleanor, Colin, Caroline, Jennifer, where is everybody? What do you all want of me? I'm telling you now that if it's the will, it isn't here."

Monica took her drink from Roger and left us in stunned

Sherbourne's Folly

silence as she stormed out of the room and upstairs. We heard her bedroom door slam.

Roger followed. I left Willow sobbing on Clive's shoulder and went to find Jennifer, who was in her room. "What was all that about, Mother? Aunt Monica was just furious so I kept out of the way." We talked for a long time; I told her about the family and Monica, that she believed somebody was unhappy with her control of the family money. "I don't know what's happening, Jennifer, but something awful is eating away at someone here and it's affecting everybody. Perhaps it's because Monica isn't too well, perhaps it makes everyone feel less stable. It's hard to imagine being here without Monica. I think it's frightening, especially for Marcus and Willow and Colin."

"But she'll be all right, Mother. Two falls and two slight heart attacks aren't the end of the world. If she would only rest perhaps she'd get over her paranoia too." We left it at that.

"Darling," I said, "let's change rooms tonight. You've had two nights of disturbed sleep, and if there is a ghost in this room maybe I can catch it."

"Oh, that seems so silly, Mother. Let's just skip it. I'll stay here."

I insisted and returned to my own room to pick up Trollope and night clothes. Jennifer departed to my room and I crawled into her bed with my book for solace.

There's a time in the night that is neither here nor there, neither day nor night, sleep or dream. Sometimes one wakes up for no apparent reason, perhaps with the sense that things aren't quite right. I woke up and lay still trying to collect my senses. I could see the vague outline of the window, the eerie light beyond it, the looming shadows of the furniture, even the outline of my body lying still in bed under the sheets. And then I saw Jennifer's ghost. I felt quite calm as I lay there looking at it through narrowed eyes. I could hear my breathing. I listened to it as I watched. The ghost did nothing but stand at the bottom of the bed for what seemed a long time. I almost fell asleep again. I wasn't threatened. A slight movement from the ghost, a shadow close by, brought my attention again. It seemed to be moving away, toward the wall. As it moved, I leaped. It didn't disappear, my arms didn't meet through a vague mist, they were wrapped around flesh and blood. We struggled in silence and I was winning, I was stronger, much stronger. I felt the body sag.

"Please don't, Jennifer, let go." The voice was Monica's. Stunned, I let go and she became one with the wall. Before she was lost I cried, "Monica." She halted and turned, shocked to hear my voice.

"What is this, Monica? What do you mean scaring Jennifer and me, what's going on? Making Jennifer a butt for Caroline's jokes. What are you up to?"

We were whispering and in this no-land light both looked like ghosts. "I'm sorry, Allison, sorry, sorry." She moved back into the room, and as she left the wall I saw the narrow opening into another space.

"Is this a secret passage?" I asked. "I didn't know we had any in this house."

"Of course we do. Several, in fact. Any house of this size built in the 1600s had secret passages." As she talked I wished I'd known about the passages when I was a child. Every child's dream. I wondered if the others knew.

"Allison, forgive me for this. I wasn't going to do it after the first night when Jennifer woke up, but then I couldn't resist."

"What do you mean, Monica. Why couldn't you resist coming in here and half scaring my daughter to death?"

"That's it, she's your daughter. I'm getting to be a lonely old woman, Allison. I love Jennifer too. I loved her parents, and since you've been here again I'm full of old memories. Please don't tell the others. I wander around a lot at night, looking and remembering."

It was the first time Monica had ever sought my conspiracy. "Of course I won't, Monica, but please don't come in and scare Jennifer again."

"I won't, darling, I won't. My mind will be elsewhere tomorrow anyway. I'm going to begin preparations for our treasure hunt. I want to do that very much."

"I'll tell Jennifer the ghost didn't show up," I said. "She can move back here tomorrow night, and she won't be disturbed again."

"Old memories," mused Monica. "It must be the onset of senility or death, bringing the worst out in me." She smiled, kissed my cheek and disappeared through her secret passage.

I wondered where else she could wander at will, secretly, through this old house. Monica seemed to have as many secrets as Snowsdown.

CHAPTER 6

The events of the last few days were conveniently forgotten. At least no one referred to Monica's fall or her accusations. Jennifer and I didn't spend much time with the family. We met them for dinner, but otherwise we roamed around the countryside, visiting nearby villages with their Norman churches and taking longer trips to Oxford and Stratford-on-Avon. Nicholas came with us that day and insisted that we drive beyond Stratford and on to Warwick so that Jennifer could see the castle. It was worth the extra hours. He was a charming young man, considerate and funny and obviously enjoying himself. He wanted to know about America.

"I've been offered a teaching appointment at Harvard," he said. "It's just for a year and I'll probably take it. I don't really know whether I really do want to teach. My father's urging me to join the firm. He has a toy factory, and I do enjoy the business side of it all."

"That doesn't seem to be an immediate problem." I smiled at him. "Why not go to America for a year. The toy factory will still be there if that's what you decide to do."

Jennifer leaned forward from the back seat. "How wonderful, I might be at Harvard next year too. I haven't decided either. And it's only two hours away from Connecticut—you can visit our home when you want to."

Warwick Castle had a ghost too. I remembered being there years ago with a party from school and the description given by the guide of secret passages, blood, revenge, ghosts; schoolgirls giggling and gasping, loving the fears and romance the history evoked. It was just the same. Jennifer, Nicholas and I were suitably impressed and awed. Although there are still living quarters in the castle, it's basically a dank old place. We were relieved to be out in the sunshine again, sitting on the lawns admiring the gardens and the peacocks who had total command of this mighty fortress.

"I haven't seen the Snowsdown ghost since you slept in my room, Mother."

"I told you, darling, I think it was exhaustion and new surroundings that prompted your fancies."

"I think you must have put the fear of God into it," she laughed. "Maybe it's haunting someone else now."

Monica hadn't referred to her nocturnal walks since we'd confronted each other in Jennifer's room. Now she was up and about, busy on the phone, gardening, talking endlessly about the treasure hunt which she'd planned for Saturday, tomorrow. The only break in her schedule was a trip to Birmingham to see Dr. Wyndham's specialist. She'd announced at dinner that there was nothing wrong with her, she'd been working too hard and needed to take it easy for a while. She had smiled at us and we had smiled, unbelieving, back at her.

"I'm so relieved," Willow offered tentatively. "Indeed yes," said Clive, his only contribution to the evening's conversation.

Roger was beaming, "Perhaps we can take a short trip

together. A quiet French village. Would you like that, Monica?"

"Yes, darling, let's do that," she said.

Caroline and Colin took great pains to be kind to Jennifer. Even Eleanor had grudgingly apologized for her tirade. It was all, on the surface, a pleasant family group. There were still tensions in the air, and Monica played on them as she discussed the treasure hunt.

"It will solve all your problems," she said looking at us as if we were conspirators in her plot. I didn't know what she was up to, but her satisfaction with the proceedings made me uncomfortable and I was not looking forward to the next day.

Fortunately, I thought, when I woke on Saturday morning, it's not raining. The event was upon us, so let's get on with it, was my reaction to it all. In a few hours it will all be over.

Caroline and Willow were in the dining room. Caroline was drinking coffee, Willow nibbling on toast and drinking tea. I helped myself to kippers and bread and butter. I missed such things in Connecticut. Kippers were available, but they didn't taste the same.

"Looking forward to it, Caroline?" I sat down opposite her.

"No, I think it's an absolute bore. I wanted to get away for the day but Mummy had a fit." She scowled at Willow.

"It's Monica's party. You can't let her down, Caroline. She insists that we all be here." Willow looked at Caroline with some exasperation. "It's just one day, one party. It won't hurt you."

Colin hadn't wanted to take part either. I'd heard him

and Roger arguing last night until finally Roger had exhausted his repertoire of love, honor, duty, Monica's sickness. Colin had finally given in and promised to take part. The rest of us were all willing to put up with Monica's whimsy, as much as we disliked it. I felt sure too that Carey would insist that Eleanor attend. And Nicholas would come because he was a polite young man and uninvolved in everybody's problems.

Monica had asked us all to keep out of her way that morning, and to keep out of the gardens because the caterers would be setting up our luncheon under Mrs. Potter's supervision. Although this was just a family affair, with Carey, Eleanor and Nicholas too, Monica wanted everything to be as elegant as it had always been in the days when there might be as many as fifty people taking part in Father's treasure hunts.

It was stunning. A small, striped marquee had been set on the lawn, and beneath its awning the food was arrayed on trestle tables covered with white cloths. Salmon, caviar, local trout, salads, tiny sandwiches of cucumber or watercress, champagne and a cool white wine, a feast that drove all thoughts of the hunt from my mind. Deck chairs were arranged in the sun or shade for those of us who didn't want to sit on the grass. As we all moved into the picnic area I felt as if I was moving onto a film stage, that Fellini might be there to call "Action, Take One." Somehow too, we had all elected to wear white clothes. Without consultation, we had agreed that white was appropriate for Monica's fantasy. The only flash of color competing with the surroundings was a green sash tied around Monica's white, straw hat, left free to float down her back. She was wearing white silk slacks and blouse, loose and flowing with her.

"Come along, darlings. Isn't it beautiful?" She swept her arms to embrace us, the occasion, the only one among us who seemed quite at ease—the rest of us were there under duress. I felt unreal, as if we were participating in a pageant but didn't know our roles yet. We were not a happy group, but Monica's enthusiasm and the food and wine, gradually eased our spirits. An hour later, lazy and full in the warm sun, we were prepared to listen to Monica's reading of the first clue.

She was flushed and looked rather grand as she stood and we remained seated looking up at her. In her hand was a piece of paper which she held up for us to see. "This is the first clue, darlings, which I shall read in just a minute. First, I want to say, I know you think that treasure hunts are frivolous—but this one is not."

Marcus groaned, "Oh do get on with it, Monica."

"Just a little patience, Marcus." She seemed suddenly nervous as she established the rules: that we must work by ourselves to solve each clue, that there were four clues and that each one would bring us a step closer to the treasure. She was mysterious and I was disconcerted by the edge of fear I felt underlying her words. I had no idea what the prize was, but it was clear that Monica was offering something that made her nervous. The treasure hunts in Father's day had been amusing; this one was riddled with intensity. It wasn't much fun.

With a great flourish Monica read the first clue:

Tarry not, leave nought to chance
The first clue leads you straight to France
Travel fast and travel light
The Frenchman's sword is not his might.

It didn't make any sense to me, or, apparently, anyone else. Caroline was the first to move, "This is stupid. Why do we have to go through this charade?"

"It's not that difficult, dear," Willow responded. "Just think about it for a minute. It's easier than the *Times* crossword I'm sure, and you're so good at that."

Roger elaborated. "It should be, anyway. The clue has to refer to something within the house and grounds, it should lead us to some place, some thing, with which we're all familiar."

Before Monica moved away toward the house she reminded us not to take the next clue when we found it, but to leave it for others to find. The object was not to eliminate everybody, but to solve the puzzle.

"Where do we find you, Aunt Monica, when we have solved it?" asked Jennifer.

"Don't worry, darling, you will." And Monica left us alone to pursue our own thoughts about clue number one.

We dispersed slowly. There was no point in staying together, we were on honor not to cheat by working together or following each other. I wandered off into the house, it was a little chillier now and a sweater would help.

It was even cooler indoors, and I raced up the stairs to my room. What could Frenchmen have to do with any of it. There were several French objects in the house. I would check the French writing desk in the study. And there was the clock Carey had given Monica years ago after a trip to Paris. There must be other things of French origin. My mind wasn't working too well and I couldn't think of them.

I ran into Jennifer as I came down to the hallway. She looked pleased with herself. "Have you worked it out already, darling?"

"Can't stop now, Mother." And she raced off.

I felt pleased with my smart daughter. How could she have worked it out so quickly? She might know about the French writing desk but surely she wasn't aware of the French clock. Perhaps I was on the wrong track, perhaps it wasn't a French item, perhaps it was a French idea.

Through the front door I saw Eleanor and Colin rushing off in different directions; she looked grim and Colin was smiling. I wondered whether they were in collusion.

Willow, looking a little confused, bumped into me as she came out of the library. "Oh, sorry, Allison." She blushed. "It's not as easy as it used to be, is it?" It was hard for me to tell from her expression whether she'd worked out the first clue or not. I thought perhaps she had as she seemed to be waiting for me to move on before she did.

"No, it's not," I smiled. "I feel as blank as when Monica first read it out to us." I went off to the study and found Roger going through the French writing desk.

He looked up, guilty. "Don't bother looking here, Allison. It's not in this desk." He turned and went on his way.

I turned to leave too and was caught for a moment by Caroline through the window. She was strolling languidly across the lawn in the direction of the maze. Whether she knew further clues or not didn't seem very important to her, her face was blank, as if there was absolutely nothing on her mind. Clive was still sitting on the lawn drinking a glass of champagne. I waved but he didn't see me.

The library. What was Willow doing there? The library, books, authors, French authors, French ideas. De Toqueville. I knew what the clue meant. I raced across the hall and into the library. No one was there. I went right to his account of his journey to America. I remembered reading it when John and I stayed here just before sailing to the States. Yes, Willow at least, had been here. The book was not pushed back into the shelf properly. I took it down and clue number two fell out onto the floor. Pushing the book back I picked up the paper:

> Continue on your way, forsooth
> This clue leads you to the truth . . .
> The truth which no man ever speaks
> To him, the loneliest of Greeks.

Diogenes. Something for everyone. Diogenes, the Greek who spent his life searching for truth, looking for light. Light. Searching. What about the lanterns used to keep off the frost from the fruit trees the other night. The shed, that's where they were. I raced off, full of joy that I'd worked it out so quickly, the third clue had to be somewhere in that shed.

Clive was still sitting on the lawn. "Aren't you hunting, Clive?" I shouted as I raced by him. "I'm not going to race around blindly." He looked up as my shadow fell across his face. "I'm going to work it out from here, then I'll go on." I left him to it.

Arriving at the shed I knew I wasn't the first on the

scene. Lanterns were strewn all over the place. It was dark in there and I almost fell over a couple of them lying just inside the door. Marcus would never have left the place looking like this. I found the switch and turned on the light. There were at least a hundred lanterns hanging around the walls from hooks. My heart sank—which one? It leaped again when I saw one that stood out. It was a regular lamp, nothing to throw off heat to keep away the frost. The only movable part was the glass face, but looking into it I could see nothing that might be a clue. I opened it anyway, puzzled for a moment, then removed the light bulb. There it was, a thin roll of paper. I withdrew it from the lamp, uncurled it and read:

> Take any path and you will find
> The answer to this clue defined
> Take any path and, amazed, we'll meet
> And ponder on my last conceit.

The paper was snatched from my hand. I jumped, turned and raised my arm defensively. It was grabbed by Eleanor. "Don't be so scared, Allison. I only want the clue."

I had been so intent upon finding the clue I hadn't heard Eleanor enter the shed. "I was already here, over there." She indicated a corner piled high with boxes. "I couldn't find the right lamp. I heard you coming and hid."

"You scared me half to death, Eleanor. And this is hardly fair."

She smiled. "It doesn't make any difference in the long run. It's one of Monica's stupid games. Anyway, I'm off now. Thanks for your help." She left me behind to roll up the clue and place it back in the lamp before I too could go off to the next rendezvous.

This one too seemed fairly obvious. Perhaps too obvious but I had to try the Folly. ". . . amazed, we'll meet" seemed to indicate the maze.

The light of the afternoon was fading as I entered the maze. Inside it was darker, hard to see with the shadows of the high hedges looming over me. I knew the formula, and it sounded easy, *go left on entering, then on the first two occasions when there is an option, go right, but then thereafter go left.* Faced with the reality of the tall hedges of the maze it is very confusing; not until you reach the core does confidence return. In the near dark it's particularly disorienting. The paths are not wide and a single shadow can throw you away from the correct turn. The last time I'd followed the path was with Monica and Jennifer a few days ago. Before that it had been when I was a young girl. I hurried along, anxious to have the whole thing done with. It had been a day of frustrations, a game Monica wanted to play. I wanted to go home, sit before the fire with a cup of tea, think about dinner and a quiet evening.

There were noises in the maze, small animals scurrying around, leaves rustling, twigs crackling, trees leaning and groaning. It was getting cold and I didn't like it. I turned left into what I thought was a path and walked into the hedge. I became caught up in its branches and struggled to get out and on my way. As I came free I stopped to catch my breath. It felt as if I was not alone. There were running footsteps, where were they? Twigs, crashing branches, a sob. I called "Who's there, who is it?" My voice trembled.

There was no answer but sudden silence. Again, I turned

to the path, began running, hopefully to the center of the maze. There was a voice and someone else's footsteps. What was the voice saying? I stopped to listen and like echoes all around me I heard the sound of someone else running in another direction, the voice playing a tune with the name. Monica, Monica, Monica, M-o-n-i-c-a, MONica, m-o-n-ICA. And then it stopped and there was silence. I waited, hearing only the sounds of my own body. A snapping twig mobilized me. My feet remembered what my head couldn't and I reached the center of the maze. The Folly. There was Monica relaxed in her white clothes, sitting on a white chair, the ribbon of her hat trailing over her shoulder and down her back. Relief, I'd arrived. Fear disappeared, here was Monica, all was well. I ran to her.

"Monica. Someone's playing games in the maze and I was terrified. What are you doing out here, are you a clue?" I giggled and ran up to her as she sat in the middle of the Folly. She didn't move. "Oh, my God." I put my hand out to touch her, pulled it back and moved to stand before her. Her head was slumped forward onto her chest, one hand rested on the arm of the chair, the other hand hung to the floor. I felt her wrist, no pulse. Her eyes had rolled back, I closed them. She was still warm. I stood and looked and didn't know where to turn, what to do. I felt the tears start down my cheeks and felt as alone as I could ever be. Gone.

Someone slipped a hand into mine. It was Willow and I remembered us as little girls standing before Monica being told that Father had died.

Her face was blotchy. "Oh, Allison. I found her just before you came. I was running off to fetch someone." She choked. "I heard you call out to Monica, and I came back."

"We must get help." I couldn't take my eyes off Monica.

"I'll go now, you stay with her." I didn't feel Willow's hand leave mine, or see her go. After a while I moved away from Monica and sat on another chair looking out into the blackness of the maze. It would be a good twenty minutes, half an hour, before Willow returned with anyone so that we could move Monica back to the house. I sat quietly alone, the lights that Monica had so discreetly arranged around the old Folly casting a glow of what might be mistaken for life upon us as they took over from the gradually sinking sun.

I don't know how long it was that I sat there with Monica. I was taken away from her death by the arrival of Colin who was just now arriving to find the next clue. It seemed like years since we'd begun this treasure hunt, that this perpetual search would go on and on until we all died. "Aunt Allison, what are you doing here? Don't you have the next clue?" He came racing into the light. "Mother, it's late, can't we pack it in for the day?" He looked at Monica, the color of his face changed from healthy glowing pink to a drained mask of white. He looked at me, stunned. My arms went around him and I felt his whole body tremble. "It must be a heart attack, dearest. Hold on." We stood together. "She would have hated it, Colin, any other way. If she could have chosen, it would be like this, quickly. No lingering illness." My words didn't convince me either but the sound of them seemed to be comforting.

And then everyone arrived. It was all a blur—Roger sobbing into Monica's lap, Nicholas and Marcus lifting her onto a wooden door they'd brought to carry her back to the house, Carey with a blanket, his face sunken, the slow walk through the maze to the house. The doctor was already there, an ambulance, the police. They asked us who had found her, when, how she had appeared. Willow was too distraught to answer their questions. I told them what I knew, how Willow had found her just before my arrival.

"There will be an autopsy," Dr. Wyndham told us. "In the case of sudden death, I'm afraid it's necessary. But not to worry, she was my patient and I'm not surprised. She tried to do too much."

Finally, it was over, everyone had left. They had taken Monica's body into Evesham. If everything was in order we could claim her tomorrow afternoon.

Mrs. Potter had gathered the remnants of lunch into the dining room and suggested we eat something. Eleanor brought Marcus a plate of food and tried to make him eat something. "Please, just a bite, darling." It was the kindest I'd ever heard her be with him. "Can I fix you something too, Roger, anyone?" We all said no and continued to sit in stunned silence.

I'd forgotten. "Where's Jennifer, where is she?" I leaped up, worried, frightened. Only now as the police and doctor left, as we all gathered together, did I realize she was missing. I hadn't even seen her since early afternoon, flooded with pride that she'd worked out the first clue.

"I saw her going to the shed ages ago," said Colin.

"She was definitely in the maze," offered Caroline, as unconcerned as ever. "We passed each other on one of the paths. She seemed to know where she was going. I was lost."

"We must find her. Come on Marcus, Clive, we must go to the maze," Nicholas spurred us all into action. "No, Mrs. Van Dyck, you stay here, she might come back. What were the other clues?"

Roger came to the center of the room. "Who went beyond the third clue? Who went beyond Monica?" None of us answered. "Where did she send Jennifer?"

No one knew but the maze seemed the place to begin. Nicholas, Marcus, Colin, Clive and Roger went out into the night. I watched them march across the lawns, the light from their lamps shining until they too became lost in the maze.

Jennifer, Jennifer. How could I have forgotten for even a moment? The voices, had she heard them, had anyone? What had Monica said to her? Monica must have been the focus of the fourth clue, why else would she be sitting in the Folly? What had she been up to? Had Jennifer found Monica dead, and distraught in her efforts to find help been lost in the maze? She would have called out, we would have heard her.

"She'll be all right, Allison." Willow patted my hand and I couldn't stand it. "You know how easy it is to get lost out there. She's probably wandering around, calling out. They'll hear her now. Don't worry." Frail, sad, aged Willow. She left the room, leaving me with Carey.

He came and sat next to me on the couch, trying to comfort me but I couldn't be still and went to sit on the front steps, peering into the darkness, urging Jennifer to come running through it and into the light. Home.

After Monica had read the first clue to us she must have gone directly to the Folly to wait. Jennifer, Willow and

Eleanor were ahead of me. Clive stayed on the lawn. Willow had found Monica's body. Eleanor said she'd waited for Marcus to catch up, she didn't know her way through the maze. Caroline was lost when she ran into Jennifer; Roger had only got as far as the lanterns. Carey, Nicholas, where were they? Where was Jennifer? She was ahead of all of us, she must have found Monica, probably talked to her, received the next clue. My head was spinning and I couldn't make sense of it all. Damn Monica's treasure hunt. Monica, dead, alone in the Folly. Monica.

It seemed like hours before they returned. Jennifer was with them, supported by Nicholas and Marcus. Her white dress was streaked black and green. Her legs were scratched, she'd lost her shoes. I saw the group emerge from the maze and raced across the lawn. Jennifer shrugged off Nicholas and Marcus and rushed into my arms. She was hysterical, frightened. "Mother, someone tried to kill me." She sobbed in heaving sighs. "Kill me." She couldn't talk and Nicholas lifted her into his arms and carried her into the house. "She needs bed and she needs a doctor." Colin went to call Wyndham again.

Nicholas stumbled along with Jennifer crying in his arms. I hung onto her hand. "It's impossible to get anything else out of her, Mrs. Van Dyck." Roger walked beside me. "We found her in the north corner, quite a way from a path out. If it hadn't been for Marcus, who seems to know every inch of that maze, I'm not sure we could have reached her so quickly."

Marcus agreed. "Fortunately, we heard her crying out. Seems like she had been unconscious for a while and woke just as we neared her. She heard our calls."

"She must have fallen," said Clive. "Easy to get lost and trip in there. A good part of that maze hasn't been touched for years. Should be closed off if you ask me."

Nicholas carried Jennifer to her room and left. I sat beside her bed waiting for Wyndham to arrive. I was worried. She was flushed and incoherent, mumbling, "Don't hurt me, please don't hit me," and saying that someone had tried to kill her. When I asked who, she couldn't answer.

Finally, Wyndham arrived. He was quiet and efficient, giving Jennifer a sedative. She fell into a deep sleep almost immediately.

"She'll be all right tomorrow, Mrs. Van Dyck. I gather she lost her sense of direction and got frightened in the maze. Let her rest tonight. She'll be fine."

I couldn't feel quite as casual as Dr. Wyndham seemed to be. By the time I joined the family in the drawing room it seemed that they too had decided to think that Jennifer had just become lost and frightened, that she tripped and knocked herself out. The idea that someone had tried to hurt her was put down to her imagination.

I was furious, upset. "You're all crazy," I screamed. "You don't want to believe anything. Monica thought someone wanted to kill her too. Well, now she's dead. Jennifer thinks someone wanted to hurt her and all you can talk about is her imagination."

"But Monica had a heart attack," cried Willow.

"I agree with you, Allison," Nicholas came and stood beside me. "Something more than a treasure hunt was going on today. What's it all about? I don't know. I do know that Monica wasn't well, but Jennifer's a young, healthy girl, not given to fancies that someone's trying to hurt her."

"If you want my opinion," Eleanor suddenly said from her seat by the window, "I think it has something to do with Jennifer, whatever's going on. I don't think Monica's recent paranoia and Jennifer's fright today are totally unconnected."

There was silence as we all looked to Eleanor, waiting for more. She didn't offer it and turned away to look out of the window again. Carey went over to his daughter. "Perhaps Eleanor is implying that it was really Jennifer who found Monica first. Perhaps that's why she ran off into the maze, frightened, became lost." He put a hand under Eleanor's elbow, "It's time we went, my dear. Come along, Nicholas."

It seemed reasonable. Tomorrow I could ask Jennifer what had happened, whether she had found Monica dead or whether she had talked to her, received the fourth clue from her. It seemed too that we would have to complete the treasure hunt, find out what it was at the end of the trail. For some reason that had to do with Monica's intensity about it all, I felt that it was important to know. Monica was dead. Dead.

CHAPTER 7

It was almost eleven o'clock when I woke the next morning and for several minutes I lay in bed savoring the quality of the day. The sun was already high in the sky, but the spring chill of a May day kept me wrapped in the warmth of the blankets. My mind was back in America with John, missing him. Then in a rush the events of yesterday. Monica's death, came surging into my head. Jennifer. I leaped out of bed, grabbed a robe and rushed down the landing to her room. Her bed was made and there was no sign of her. She must be feeling much, much better. I was ashamed that on this morning I had not been awake early enough to talk with Jennifer, to help, to find out what had happened to her. And Monica, funeral arrangements. I was overwhelmed with sadness and depression, fear or not knowing what was happening and, that whatever it was, there was no time to think. Event and horror were piled one upon the other.

Everyone was up, the house, unlike Monica, alive.

"Just like you, Allison, sleeping when we need help." I was greeted by a pale Willow. She still looked drained, agonized, exhausted.

"I'm sorry. Where's Jennifer?"

"I haven't seen her." She turned back to the writing desk

where she was making a list. "But there can't be much wrong with her. She's gone riding with Colin again."

I poured some coffee. "What are you doing, Willow?"

"Well somebody's got to prepare the invitation list for the funeral. I've talked to the Vicar, and the service will be held on Tuesday at noon."

Roger was in Evesham, gaining release of Monica's body. Wyndham had seemed to think there would be no problem; as far as he could tell the cause of death was a heart attack. I wished that I had been up in time to go with him. It would be a terrible ordeal for him alone, the legal procedures, making arrangements for Monica to be returned to Lower Pershing.

"Will her body be brought back here, Willow?"

"Not until tomorrow night when she'll be taken by hearse to the church. We can go and see her then."

I wanted to scream at Willow's lists, her practical mind, the calmness with which she approached the funeral arrangements. No more Monica, no more laughing in this house. I wanted to go home. But I accepted quietly Willow's suggestion that I help Caroline and Clive making phone calls and sending telegrams to advise Monica's friends, acquaintances and colleagues that she had died. With all the incoming calls from London, Oxford and even Europe, it was an almost impossible task to be efficient, working quickly down the lists that Willow gave us. Newspapers and television stations called and asked tedious questions, confirmation of facts already in their files. I became caught up in all the activity, almost forgetting what it was all about, almost enjoying the excitement. My new mood was diminished when Roger returned from Evesham.

His face was drawn, his eyes red, he was an old man. "I've got to go back to Evesham this afternoon. To select a coffin and make the arrangements with the mortician."

"Let me come with you, Roger." He looked at me gratefully.

"I'd like that, Allison."

Monica's body would be released later in the day. After we'd talked with the funeral people, Roger and I could go back to the mortuary, he would sign a release and everything would be in order.

"There were some bruises on Monica's shoulders and the back of her neck," he said. "She suffered a massive heart attack. Wyndham and the coroner agree that the bruises were from the fall downstairs, the strain of that was the real prelude to this attack. Preparing for the treasure hunt was no help. Too much excitement."

We were driving to Evesham when Roger gave me the details, the official cause of death. "Did you know she had leukemia, Allison?" He turned to looked at me. I couldn't deny that I had known and I could see the pain in his eyes. "Why didn't she tell me, why?"

"She didn't want to worry you." Even to me this sounded inadequate.

"Dammit," he banged his fist against the steering wheel and the car skewed across the road. "I was worried anyway. Falls, heart attacks. I knew she wasn't well. I've been worried to death. I could have taken care of her."

"That's why she didn't tell you, Roger. She didn't want to be taken care of, treated like an invalid. I think she only told me because I don't belong here any more, and it may have helped for her to say once, out loud, 'I'm dying.' Don't be angry with her now, Roger."

We drove in silence for a long time, both of us thinking of Monica, the difference in our lives. Roger broke the silence by asking about Jennifer. I still hadn't seen her, and I was worried. She had been so frightened last night. Whatever it was, it had been very real to her. Jennifer was very different than Monica, so why she should believe, as her aunt had, that someone was trying to kill her?"

"Monica was always strange about Jennifer," he said apologetically. "I don't know how to explain it except that she was always terribly interested in her successes. You know she had more photographs of her around the house than she ever had of Colin, or any of us."

I was surprised. I hadn't seen any photographs. She'd apparently taken them all down before we arrived. As Monica had said to Roger, "Who needs pictures when the real thing is here?"

He didn't remember Jennifer's real parents, only Monica's sadness at their death, which had happened before he and Monica married.

He was reflective. "I wonder what Eleanor meant last night when she said something about Jennifer's fright and Monica's paranoia?"

I didn't know either. Ever since we'd arrived events and feelings had been off-key in some indefinable way. Monica's preoccupation with the treasure hunt had somehow brought it all together. There was something wrong. Whatever it was, it had affected all of us in uncomfortable private ways.

Selecting a coffin for Monica was an ordeal but it was fast. Simple oak, silver fittings, a white lining and the funeral director hadn't tried to push anything on us; had retired to allow Roger and me to make our own decisions. It was painful but didn't begin to prepare us for the mortuary. Roger and I were led down endless institutional green corridors to the cold room. Monica had to be identified before the papers could be signed. "You don't have to come, Allison." Roger took my arm and tried to lead me to a seat in the waiting room. But I couldn't do that. I wanted to see Monica—no, I didn't want to see Monica—I *had* to see her.

I had never seen a body before. In England coffins are rarely left open for viewing, and in America I had never taken the opportunity to view the bodies of the two or three people I'd known who'd died. I was frightened. Monica lay there and I couldn't take my eyes away from her, couldn't resist putting a finger to her cheek, feeling its coldness. It didn't convince me that she was dead—reconciling the reality before me and my memory wasn't a natural, automatic event. I left in shock and, finally, in the car with Roger driving home to Lower Pershing, sobbed. By the time we swept into the driveway it was over and I thought I could live with Monica's importance in my life, and her death.

Jennifer was in the library, a chair pulled up to the fire, a light over her shoulder, reading. She looked tired but there was a healthy glow to her cheeks and she smiled as I walked over to her.

I called to Mrs. Potter and asked her to bring us tea. It was my favorite time of day. The light outside was fading, the single light and the glow from the fire was comforting. A book, tea, a companion and a wonderful sense of security. I was sad that Jennifer and I couldn't just sit there relishing our comfort, that too many things were happening to make that possible. Until tea was served we allowed ourselves the illusion that all was well with our world and talked about Jennifer's ride with Colin and how good it made her feel, how incredibly lovely the countryside was. I didn't mention my trip to Evesham with Roger.

"I feel so stupid about yesterday, Mother. I didn't know until I got up this morning that Aunt Monica had died. Colin told me, that's why the horses were ready and we spent the day away."

My heart filled with warmth and love for Colin, that in the midst of his own unhappiness, he'd thought of Jennifer. They'd ridden hard and later talked. He'd told Jennifer about growing up with Monica, how he'd always resented her trips abroad, her interests which went so far beyond him; and how he'd admired her, boasted about her to his friends. And now he was sad that he'd never known her. "I felt that we were just reaching a point where we could be friends, adults together and that perhaps soon we could really talk to each other," he'd said. And he'd cried as they drove the horses once more across the fields.

"But, darling, what happened to you yesterday? I was terrified when you didn't return. And you were hysterical when you were found." We sat and looked at each other and I saw the color fade from her cheeks and some emotion that I couldn't define, cloud her eyes.

"Someone chased me through the maze, then hit me on the neck and knocked me unconscious," she said, terror in her quiet voice. She was so sure; I believed her. "Tell me exactly what happened, from the time we ran into each other in the hall outside the library."

She *had* found the clue and was running off to the shed to search through the lanterns. In normal circumstances she would have had difficulty with that clue, but the frost earlier in the week had put the lanterns very clearly into her mind. It hadn't taken more than a few minutes to find the right lamp. Clue in hand she'd rushed off to the Folly. "I didn't know where to look, or what to expect when I got there, but I knew the clue couldn't refer to any other place." She'd remembered the directions from our first visit, and within a very short time arrived at the center of the maze. Monica was there, waiting.

"You're the first, Jennifer," she'd said. "I always imagined you would be quick-minded."

"She was very strange, Mother, very sad." Jennifer interrupted her story.

"What do you mean, dear?"

She insisted that Jennifer sit with her for a moment, saying that it would take the others a few minutes to catch up. "I like sitting here with you, Jennifer. I wish . . ." and she didn't continue.

"What do you wish, Aunt Monica? Does it have something to do with the treasure hunt?"

"In a circuitous way it does, my dear." She paused and gazed off into the maze and seemed to drift for a moment. "Do you ever wonder about your real parents, Jennifer?" she asked. "They were romantics, both of them, but your mother was too pragmatic for her own good."

She wouldn't elaborate but proceeded to give her the

next clue. It wasn't written down this time and Monica repeated it twice. Jennifer struggled trying to recall it. It took a moment, but she hadn't forgotten:

> For you the race is almost won
> Rest not but go where rest is done
> There volumes can tell you much
> And gates will open at your touch.

Jennifer hadn't understood it, but Monica had urged her on. I didn't understand it either and didn't want to stop Jennifer's story to think about it.

"When you come to the end of the trail, Jennifer, you'll know about your parents," Monica said. "They were very close to me."

Jennifer had moved slowly away from the Folly. "I heard someone else approaching from the other side of the maze as I went on my way," she said. "I don't know who it was."

Since she didn't understand the clue and, believing she knew how to work her way out of the maze, she decided to stop on one of the side paths, to sit and think about it for a while. And that's when the terror began. She sat on the stump of a tree for a few minutes, but it was chilly and she decided to move on. And then she heard a noise on her left. "Who is it?" she called but no one answered. She began to make her way back to what she thought was the main path. She heard footsteps, underbrush being trampled behind her. She began to run, and then she heard the voice. "Monica, Monica, Monica, M-o-n-i-c-a, MONica, m-o-n-ICA." I caught my breath, I'd forgotten. "What, Mother, what is it?"

"I heard it too, darling. It scared me, and I ran too." I

wondered whether we had heard the voice at the same time, whether we had been that close to each other.

Her next sentence convinced me that it hadn't been at the same time. "And then there was laughter, crazy, panting laughter." I had heard a sob and as Jennifer continued I thought it might be the same person, but later, after he or she had knocked Jennifer down.

She ran and the voice kept floating behind her, the footsteps were getting closer, seeming to come from all around her. Jennifer kept changing paths, blindly trying to run from her pursuer, getting lost. She tripped over a fern, got up and ran on, but before she could turn to confront her assailant, she was hit viciously with some kind of club at the base of her skull, and knocked unconscious.

"The next thing I knew Marcus was calling my name. It was dark, and I was lying on the ground thinking I could never get up, and I was scared. At first I didn't even want to call out to Marcus—maybe it had been him who was chasing me."

I looked at Jennifer's neck. The bruise at the base of it wasn't imagination. Someone had hit her and violently. But who? Why?

"Did you tell Colin all this, Jennifer?"

"No, I didn't feel much like talking this morning. We were both preoccupied with Aunt Monica's death."

"Well don't, darling. Let's worry about this ourselves. If anyone asks you about it, just say you were scared and probably babbling because of Aunt Monica's own fantasies about being pushed downstairs. Okay?"

She agreed. "But what do you think it's about, Mother? I don't want to stay here."

"Just a little longer, sweetheart. We'll spend time together, just don't go wandering off by yourself. It's curious that Monica asked you about your real parents. I think I'm going to have to find out more about this myself."

I might even have to go down to Dunster to check the records. Or perhaps there would be something in Monica's room.

Dinner was a subdued affair. Exhausted after his unbearable day, Roger didn't join us. Mrs. Potter took a tray to his room, and later I saw her take it back to the kitchen untouched. It was, strangely, the only moment of peace we'd had together all day. Mrs. Potter served the soup, set the roast and vegetables on the sideboard and retired to answer phone calls and take messages. Everyone we could think of had been notified, the announcements of the service put in the local, Birmingham and London papers. It was going to be a big funeral, and we doubted that the local church would accommodate everyone who came.

"What about the solicitor? Has anyone notified Selby?" asked Colin.

Willow nodded. "I called him first thing this morning. He was shocked and very upset. He's coming up from London for the services."

Caroline moved to serve herself at the sideboard. "What about the will, does he have that?"

Clive was shocked. "That's nothing for you to discuss, Caroline, it'll all be taken care of at the appropriate time."

"Selby talked to Roger, and I gather asked him to check Monica's personal effects, her papers. He does have a will but wants to be absolutely sure that it's not superseded by a later one," said Willow. "He's coming tomorrow evening,

Sherbourne's Folly

will spend the night at The Bell, and will attend the funeral on Tuesday morning. Afterward he'll read the will."

There was silence with this piece of information. Caroline came back to the table, "I wonder where it's all going."

For the first time Marcus looked around at us. "You make me sick, all of you. It's out of our hands. Surely you can wait two days to find out what your shares are." He stormed from the room. He was devastated by Monica's death and had spent the day alone tramping over the land. I had the feeling he'd taken his flask along too, that it was all he could do to hold himself together. I wondered where Eleanor had been all day, why she wasn't with Marcus.

I found him after dinner sitting in Monica's room. I'd checked his first, found it empty and cold. On a whim I turned the handle to Monica's room, opened the door to see Marcus sitting in her chair, a glass in one hand, the other covering his eyes. He was crying. I put my arms around him and I felt the sobs in his body. We held each other for a long time until finally he stopped shaking. It's curious how feelings repeat themselves. As we sat there I remembered Marcus going off to school for the first time. He'd sobbed then and I'd held him, feeling the sobs racking his body just as they were now. My baby brother, Marcus. I loved him very much.

"'I can't stand it, Allison. What's happening here? What will we do without Monica?"

"You'll be all right, Marcus. Monica has depended on *you* for so many years. You've made this place successful, profitable. Monica couldn't have done that."

"I'm going to miss all those fights we used to have,

though. Every time I've wanted to make an improvement, do something different, she's nagged and made me thoroughly explore the ideas. That's why it's worked. I'm not sure I can do it by myself."

"Of course you can. You and Eleanor can make it work for both of you." I took his glass away and made us both fresh drinks from Monica's cabinet.

"Eleanor." He shook his head. "I don't know what's happening to us, either. Until recently she was good for me, we were good together, supportive. But now I feel resentment and anger from her."

"You know what I think about that, Marcus? That you've always wanted Eleanor to be Monica. She too is a strong woman, dynamic, beautiful, but you've tried to force her into the mold of Snowsdown, not allowed her her own life with you. What do you think the stables are all about? Her unwillingness to live here?"

As I said it, it suddenly seemed true. It was a new thought for Marcus too. "You don't like her, do you, Allison? No one does very much. But she always brought joy into my life."

I had never liked Eleanor, but that didn't blind me to her relationship with Marcus. And he needed someone strong and forthright—and Eleanor certainly was that.

"She called earlier, and came by. I avoided her." He looked embarrassed. "I think I'll call her now."

Alone in Monica's room I looked around. It was a good time to look for some information about Jennifer's parents, perhaps even the will. The only right I had to invade her private affairs was the right I felt to protect my daughter, to find out what had scared her and whether, in fact, Monica could have been pushed downstairs or whether it was all in her imagination. Putting my guilty hesitations aside, I opened the top drawer of her desk. It was full of photographs of Jennifer. Roger was right, there were dozens of them. Jennifer as a baby, on her first tricycle, going off to school, in the church choir, playing hockey and tennis, standing in front of our house, waving from the car. Pictures of trips and friends and events of her young life. With a start, I realized I was wasting time mulling over them. Pushing them back I closed the drawer.

There was nothing much to be found in any of the other drawers. A few insurance forms, letters, bills, her checkbook, but nothing important. Nothing from the past. I wondered whether Monica's room *had* been searched when she accused us the other night of wanting her dead, and if it had been searched, had anything been stolen.

The door opened and Willow came into Monica's room. I jumped, startled and guilty.

"What are you doing, Allison?"

"I've been talking to Marcus. He just left to call Eleanor. I was just thinking of going to bed. What are you doing here?"

"Looking for you," she said. "It's going to be awful around here for the next few days, maybe it'll never be any better. I thought perhaps we could relax together for a while, to talk."

"Anything special?" I sat in Monica's chair and picked up my drink.

Willow's interest in talking was surprising. We hadn't had one conversation since I'd arrived. She was always bustling around, taking care of Monica, worrying about Caroline. She looked unhappy and harried. She had always been that way though, closed off, never finding time—or perhaps anything very much—to laugh about.

"I'm feeling sad and old tonight," she said. "Things are going to change without Monica. I don't know what's going to happen to this house, whether Clive and I should move here."

I was aghast. "That's ridiculous, Willow. The house will be Colin's or Roger's. If anybody lives here it will be them. Or Marcus and Eleanor. You have your house in London."

"But this is my home," she began to sob.

I hadn't realized how strongly she felt about Snowsdown. My own home was in Connecticut with John and Jennifer. I had assumed that Willow thought of her home in London with Clive and Caroline. Of course, they'd all spent a lot of time here, holidays and vacations, year after year.

"What about Clive's business, your home in London?" I handed her a tissue.

"I like having the house there too," she said. "But this is home, this is where I grew up, where I want Caroline to be married from. This is not an insignificant house. We do not have a trivial background, we have a position. I'm part of that. I just want it to stay in the family."

"It'll be here for you, Willow." I held out my hand to her. "Why don't you go to bed now? It's been a long day for all of us, and there will be more of them coming. I'll try to help as much as I can."

We left Monica's room together and at her door, hugged each other. "Good night, Willow. You won't lose your home. None of us will."

She closed her door quietly and I found my own bed.

CHAPTER 8

Forty-eight hours ago Monica was alive, and now she's dead. I wondered how long it would be before I would forget, just for a moment, the pain the thought of not being with her any more brought. I spent the morning writing to John in Connecticut, pouring out my memories of Monica and my confusion about the animosities and bitterness I felt from the others about the will. I couldn't bring myself to tell him that someone had hit Jennifer on the head or that Monica had thought one of us had wanted her dead. Although I was determined to get to the bottom of it all, I didn't want to believe it. I hadn't believed Monica, but the truth of the bump on Jennifer's head was real and I was frightened. And angry. It was an anger that surged inside me so that I could hardly think coherently and couldn't speak to any one else without suspicion and resentment. I had to carry on through Monica's funeral and the reading of the will. I had to watch them all. I had to find out about the treasure hunt, where the final clue would lead. That I thought must be the answer to everything.

I would go back to the Folly and think about it there. Was it more than fancy that focused Monica's treasure hunt around the Folly? Was the final answer there?

I sealed the letter to John and wished that I were on my

way too. I left it on the hall table for Mrs. Potter to drop off later in the village. Turning, I was startled by Monica's white hat hanging on the wooden coat stand. It was there, green ribbon trailing, waiting to be worn. I took it down and put it on my own head, fixing it firmly into place with the long, silver-tipped, hat pin skewered on its brim. I was not used to wearing hats so it felt strange on my head, and the reflection in the mirror confirmed my feeling.

"What are you doing wearing that?" It was Willow. Lost in my own thoughts, I hadn't heard her enter the hall. She sounded cross and I tore it off my head.

"Missing Monica," I said. "Why is it hanging here? Shouldn't it be put away in her room?"

"Give it to me," and she took it out of my hands. "I can't do everything at once, you know." She moved on up the stairs and left me standing there looking at myself in the mirror.

The front door opened and Marcus came in. He was smiling. "You look awfully cheerful in this house of gloom." I turned to greet him.

"I just left Eleanor, we've been walking around and talking. You know, I think you might be right about her strength and how I've tried to make her like Monica. I told her what you'd said."

She hadn't said much in response but laughed and said, "Allison may be right. Why don't you and I try and find out who we are now," and taken his arm as they'd walked together. Marcus looked like a different man this morning, the first sign of relief that Monica's death might bring to several members of the family.

Seeing his relaxed and almost cheerful face, I realized I

didn't want to go out to the Folly alone. I told him Jennifer's clue.

"I'm no good at those clues, Allison. I only got to first base the other day. I'd keep you company, but why don't you give Carey a ring? He'd be much more helpful."

He was right. Carey was good at puzzles. Feeling more light-hearted I called him on the phone. He sounded tired yet pleased to hear from me. No one had seen him yesterday. When Roger had called asking him to spend the day with the family he'd refused, saying he preferred to spend it quietly by himself. He was part of our family, his loss was as great as ours, but we all handled it in our own ways.

I poured some coffee in the dining room and took it into the drawing room while I waited for Carey and thought about what it would be like without Monica. Even though I lived in America I had received hundreds of postcards from her over the years. She rarely had time to write letters, but wherever she traveled there was a card telling us what she was doing and asking about our lives. I wrote her long letters, she would respond with another postcard. Willow and Marcus had always been under her thumb and on her doorstep. When Monica thought it was time, and Willow hadn't done anything about finding a husband, Monica found Clive, introduced him to Willow and married them off in no time. Although it had worked out for them I had the feeling that they'd both just been weaker than Monica and neither of them had had anything better to do.

Marcus had been held by the land and his feeling that there was nothing else for him to do. Monica had certainly encouraged his intellectual inferiority by always saying things like, "Oh, Marcus loves the land, hates to sit down with a book." We'd just assumed she was right. Marcus hadn't disagreed.

Roger was in his own world, with his books and birdwatching. He wasn't interested in controlling anybody or giving advice. He'd been taken care of, and he enjoyed paying attention to Monica, basking in her fame and family and seemed perfectly happy.

I felt sure too that Colin and Caroline had been as directed as any of us. It was hard to know the effect, whether they had learned to stand up for themselves or whether they would go along with Monica's stronger will. Colin was a friendly, warm, sensible young man, but Caroline was already cynical and bitter.

"There you are, my dear." It was Carey coming into the room. "I let myself in. No one answered the door." He looked weary and I rose in greeting. Hugging him I felt his frail body and felt that if I pressed too hard he would snap in two. He was pleased by my affection, and I was reminded of how little we all touched each other to show that we cared.

I found my coat and we set off for the Folly. I wasn't looking forward to being there again but felt driven to work out Jennifer's clue. I took Carey into my confidence.

"But why would anyone frighten Jennifer or hit her on the head? It doesn't make sense." He was shocked and I could tell didn't believe it was true.

"You would if you saw the bump on the back of her head." I was angry, I hadn't considered that Carey would be as skeptical about Jennifer's fear as I had been about Monica's.

"She's at my house with Nicholas at the moment," he said. "She seems in good form, they're playing table tennis.

"But have you thought," he continued, "that Jennifer found Monica dead, became frightened and ran off into the maze? She could have fallen and forgotten."

It wasn't entirely implausible, but I didn't believe it. "She has the clue, though. Monica gave it to her."

"I wish I knew why the treasure hunt had been so important to Monica," he said. "She kept saying that it was important to all of us, insisting that it was something we all wanted."

"I don't think it was just a whim either." I didn't tell him that at the back of my mind was the thought that it had something to do with her will. She had seemed so sure that someone was after her money, that someone had been in her room searching for something—perhaps the will. It wasn't supposed to be a complicated will, but no one was sure how it would break down. Was there something in it that threatened us? It was all so vague in my mind that I would have felt silly sharing my thoughts about it with Carey. Also, I doubted the advisability of talking about the family, suggesting things that probably weren't true.

Reaching the center of the maze was always unexpected. To move from high hedges and darkness into a square of light, with this curious white building in the middle of it, was a surprise. It had never failed to delight me, to make me smile. But this time as Carey and I rounded the last hedge and I saw it before us, I felt only a grimness that I knew would be a long time in disappearing whenever I thought of the Folly. The chair in which Monica had been sitting when I found her was still there and I couldn't see it without thinking of her.

I wanted to leave. "This is a futile trip, Carey. Let's go."

He took my arm. "No, Allison. The clue began here. Even if we don't know where it leads, it seems to be the best place to think about it. There must be some reason why Monica chose this as the place to pass on the fourth and final clue."

"The others were written down for all of us to find," I said. "I wonder why Monica passed the last one on verbally?"

We sat on a shared tree stump and looked away from the Folly into the maze. It was chilly and Carey put his arm around my shoulders. He was very still and I asked him what he was thinking. "About Monica, my dear. She was at her loveliest when I last saw her. We talked about Greece, held hands, she gave me the clue and I went on my way."

"She gave you the clue too?" I was stunned. "Why didn't you say so before? I thought Jennifer was the first here, the only one to be given that clue."

"Why did you assume that, Allison?" His arm loosened on my shoulder as he turned to look at me.

"Well, you didn't mention it, and from what everybody else said about their movements, I assumed that was so." Suddenly excited, I jumped up to look at him. "Do you know the answer, did you follow it through?"

Carey sat there and looked up at me. "Well, I did work something out, but I'm still puzzled. The clue led me back to Monica's room, a copy of Mary Renault's *The Bull from the Sea* on her bookshelf and inside the book dozens of snapshots of Jennifer, crammed between its pages."

Confused, I sat down again. "What? Why pictures of Jennifer? I don't understand how that clue led to Monica's room." Were they the photographs I'd seen in Monica's desk?

"It seemed fairly straightforward to me," he said,

> Go back with me to ancient days
> Go back to labyrinthine ways
> Aegeus knew him by his sword
> He fought and slew the Minotaur.

"Not to me, Carey. First of all that's not the clue Jennifer was given, and I don't understand a word of that one either."

Suddenly he looked embarrassed and I saw some knowledge pass over his face. "I'm stupid, Allison. That clue was for me. Jennifer's was for her. What was it?"

I told him and his face looked as blank as my mind felt. "What was Monica up to?" he said. "Did she have a different clue for each of us?"

"Let's go and ask everyone." I jumped up.

He held my hand. "As far as we know no one else was here speaking to Monica. Let's wait a minute and think about this."

I pulled my hand from his, became very still as everything fell into place and I asked with a cold, knife-edge to my voice, "Just what were you and Monica doing in Greece? Why all those pictures of Jennifer? What does your clue add up to, Carey?"

"We fell in love there, Allison. We had an affair." He

was pale, subdued and beaten. My impulse to attack him died. He was an old man. He held his hands out toward me and took a step. "Afterward I was worried, Allison. When she came back to England I asked Monica if everything was all right. She said yes. There was Roger and Jessica, and we never talked about it again. It was hard to hear his voice, he turned away and wrapped his arms across his chest, hugging his memories to himself. "It feels like a dream—it was all a dream."

Unable to control my anger, I pulled him around to face me again. "It's not a dream, Carey, not a dream. There's Jennifer, my daughter." And I burst into tears. He moved toward me, "Don't touch me, Carey, go away."

He moved back to the tree stump, sat down and lit a cigarette. I stood and cried away my anger. Monica was Jennifer's mother; Carey, her father. Why hadn't Monica told me years ago? Why the pretense about a friend named Maggie Davis? The deceit. I felt that if she was alive I'd kill her myself. Roger, Jessica, me, John, Carey and, most of all, Jennifer. It was a long time, but gradually I calmed and began to realize that someone else must have suspicions about Jennifer's birth. Her existence as Monica's daughter could change the will. It would certainly change our lives.

"Carey," I moved to sit beside him, "this whole treasure hunt, this farce, was some plan of Monica's to tell us all that she was Jennifer's mother. She's dead, but you and I have found out, so please let's be careful. I don't want to tell Jennifer yet." What would I say? Why, why did she do it? How could I bear to tell Jennifer? "I want to find out what's going on before I do."

He held me close. My daughter's father comforted me. "I won't, Allison. I dread it too, and yet we probably shall have to. It's not something we should keep secret, even if no one else knows. We'll find out about Monica's plans together. It has to be all right."

I didn't think Carey would be much help, although he did have family information, twenty years I didn't know anything about. I was aware of his pain, how shocked and upset he must be to discover, suddenly, that he had a grown daughter, a young woman whose life was totally foreign to him.

"After all this time, Allison, if I could have wished anything, it is that Jennifer's true parentage remain a secret." He smiled and seemed younger in the half light filtering through the trees. "I know it has little to do with me any more, Jennifer is your daughter, but you know, I'm getting used to the idea of knowing. Jennifer's special in the way Monica was, the way you are. There's something of me now in your family that can never go away."

On the way back to the house we talked a little bit about Jennifer's clue. I had a vague idea that I wanted to test out later, but I didn't want to talk to Carey about it. Drained and exhausted we walked most of the way in silence. My feelings for Carey were mixed, I was going through some new understanding and adjustment. My feelings for Monica were clear. I was angry, wanted to hit out at her. How dare she offer Jennifer to us and now suddenly take her back. Would we never be rid of her presence? I hated her.

John and I had never had a proper birth certificate for Jennifer. Monica said she would mail it when it came through from Somerset. And then she said it was lost.

We'd had a new one drawn up in America when Jennifer began school and it seemed that some official might need to see it. I intended to find a copy of the original.

Carey left me at the door. I went to my room, lay down and fell fast asleep. It was dark when I awoke but I felt much better, clearer about what was happening, what I must do. It was going to be difficult but I would keep my own counsel, behave as normally as possible with my family and watch them all very closely.

"Mother, are you sleeping?" It was Jennifer knocking at the door. Infinitely the most difficult confrontation of my life would be seeing her, now. If I could pull this off, I knew I could handle the rest of the family with ease.

"Come in, darling, I've just been resting."

I was momentarily overwhelmed by the thought of it all and reached out to hug her. "Let go, Mother, I can't breathe." I laughed, letting her go, feeling by her reprimand just like a mother. "Sorry, Jen. It's an exhausting, traumatic time, and it felt good to see you walk in the door."

"I was worried. I came back from Carey's house ages ago." She grinned. "I beat Nicholas *and* Eleanor at table tennis. They invited us both back later. Will you come?"

I agreed and then told her about walking with Carey, trying to think of a solution to the clue Monica had given her. As we talked I watched her closely, and began to see for the first time Carey and Monica as her parents. She had inherited their lean, tall bodies and their elegance. I realized then that she was going to be an extraordinarily beautiful woman. She had the beginnings of great style, the mind and power to bring it all together. John and I had raised her, trained her mind, taught her the things we believed in, but she had inherited the innate qualities of her biological parents. Strangely, it didn't make me feel less like her mother. I began to feel that I liked this new information, and it pleased me that I had always, until now, loved and admired her parents.

"I can't solve it either, Mother. I'm stumped. It looks as if we're no closer now than we were yesterday. I feel so stupid." She thumped her fist against the wall, then looked shame-faced. "I'm sorry, but it's awful around here and I do have a bump on my head. If it wasn't for that, I wouldn't believe anything."

If Jennifer's clue was as personal as Carey's, she must have a key somewhere in her mind to unlock the puzzle. I had a feeling that I might know more about it than Jennifer, but it was too soon to talk to her about it.

"I'm going away for the day tomorrow, Jennifer. I'll be up and out early. When the others ask, tell them I needed a day off and went to London."

She was upset when I wouldn't tell her where I was going, but I asked her to trust me, that I needed to work something out in my own way.

"All right, Mother, if you say so," and good-naturedly she linked her arm through mine and we went off to confront the rest of the family. At least I'd awakened in time for tea.

We drove over to Carey's house after dinner. Marcus came with us. It was a relief to be out of Snowsdown. Occasionally we caught ourselves relaxing and laughing and I felt guilty. Monica was not even buried and here we were scurrying off. As I thought of her my anger and sorrow at her death caught up with me and my somber moments would catch Marcus and Jennifer as they chatted about other things. Carey spent the evening in his study, and the evening with Nicholas and Eleanor was full of somber moments. Someone would comment on something and we would be reminded of Monica, caught in the middle of conversation—even laughter—and suddenly feel like crying. It was a schizophrenic release, a renewing to get through the next few days.

Eleanor was still cool and snappish, but sometimes she too forgot her usual manner and enjoyed herself. She was freer with me and Jennifer. To Marcus she was loving and seemed happy that he was there with her.

Nicholas was attentive to Jennifer and especially attentive to me. I enjoyed watching his interest in my daughter who was really his second cousin. Finally, I laughed at his contortions. "Relax, Nicholas. You're like a yo-yo and it makes me feel very old. I might be Jennifer's mother but I'm not at the point where I like to be fussed over because of it. Come on, let's play that game of table tennis." He didn't fuss at all and I beat him two games out of three. I liked the game. We didn't talk much and the rhythm of bouncing balls against the table and paddles was soothing. Afterward I left him to Jennifer with Marcus as umpire. Eleanor and I left them and went to sit before the fire with coffee.

Eleanor had played with us when we were children; she was an only child and always included in our family plans. We had discovered our passion for horses and riding together, and for several years we'd all shared a rather slow, ancient pony we called Dolly. We all said we wanted horses of our own, but Eleanor was the one who worked at odd jobs on the land with the laborers picking fruit and saving her money to buy one. My passion for a horse diminished when I was about fourteen. Eleanor's increased. We gradually began to see less of her and, with the freedom of adolescence, began to form different friendships. It was to be many years before she and Marcus became engaged and she again became closely connected with our family. As we sat before the fire with our coffee I could still see the determined young girl who had finally and triumphantly ridden over to Snowsdown on her own horse. She didn't need us any more.

"Marcus told me what you said, Allison, about his trying to fit me into his image of Monica." Her face, glowing from the fire, was reflective and sad as she said in a quiet, precise voice, "I'm not going to miss her at all, I'm glad she's dead." She looked at me expecting some response. When I remained quiet, not shocked or surprised by her comment, she continued, "I've hated what she's done to Marcus, to all of them. You were lucky getting away, going to America, keeping your myths intact."

"What do you mean, myths?"

"Well, you still believe that Monica was God's gift to humanity." She grinned as I, about to deny it, laughed and agreed.

"But we all have felt that way, Eleanor."

"No," she disagreed. "You all used to think that, but you're the only believer left—and perhaps Roger."

"But she was an unusual, remarkable woman," I said.

"She was a presence we all couldn't help adoring. She was rare and magic."

"That was only one side of her." Eleanor reached for glasses and moved to the sideboard to fix us drinks. "She was also narrow, frightened and could be very cruel. You know, don't you," she came back, handed me a glass and stood looking down at me, "that she and Father had an affair when they were in Greece all those years ago?" She sat down, all the time watching my face. "Yes, I see you did know." I didn't tell her I'd only just found out.

"How did you know, Eleanor?" I asked.

She sipped from her drink. "Years ago I found some letters in the attic. They're not there any more. I was eighteen when I first found them. I didn't want to think about it, so I put it all out of my mind, and replaced the letters. A few years ago I went to get them out again and they were gone." She stared into the fire and I saw the younger Eleanor, the shock and horror she would have felt.

"My mother was still alive when they met each other in Greece. The letters from Monica were passionate and left no doubt that their affair had been physical. I couldn't bear it. It's still difficult for me to think of Father and Monica." Embarrassed, she lit another cigarette. "The letters traced the course of their relationship from passion to its disintegration and ultimately Monica's desertion of Father. He was prepared to divorce my mother," her voice had risen and I could feel the pain she still felt, "to marry Monica." Eleanor had adored Jessica, lovely, gentle Jessica lying ill for ten years before death brought her release and loneliness for Eleanor.

"Monica turned him down. In the first letter about marriage she wrote kindly but firmly that her work was important. Then her letters became angry, saying she didn't love Father, that all they'd had was a summer romance. She was going to marry Roger."

Her voice was low and I felt very close to her. It was hard to believe that Eleanor and I were really having this conversation. She looked at me, "There was only one letter after that, it was a condolence to Father on the death of Mother."

I stared at her hardly knowing what to say. "Eleanor, you said Monica was frightened. What did you mean?"

"She was frightened of everybody leaving her. I think she pulled all those strings surrounding herself with all the problems because she was afraid that she wouldn't be loved, needed. I think she thought that the only thing holding everyone together was money and power, and so she controlled both, and all of you."

"That was strength, Eleanor, not fear," I said, finding it hard to listen to Eleanor's evaluation of Monica.

She disagreed, "Just look what she's done to your family, Allison. Marcus belittled by Monica's management. He's the one who made that farm work, but Monica made sure all the credit came to her. And Willow, a frightened shadow bustling about picking up after Monica, a perfect mate for Clive who is so stupid he thinks Willow's the perfect wife. He doesn't see that Monica made her into everybody's housekeeper. Caroline is Willow's only passion, and Caroline hates her, hates Monica, everybody. Colin seems to be holding his own, but perhaps, like Roger, he doesn't care. Roger lives in some ivory tower where nothing—no emotion, no interest beyond some local birds, no concern about anybody—touches him. They're all failures at living. Now that Monica's dead the chances are that they'll build up her legend—it's safer, it's secure and it will prevent them from thinking about their own lives."

Her voice had risen angrily and she stalked around the room. "And look what it's done to me and Marcus. We've been engaged five years and, while Monica never actually said anything to discourage an early marriage, she certainly hasn't encouraged Marcus to make any moves. He's been torn by both of us. I dropped out about two years ago and have merely gone through the motions of being his fiancée. I couldn't fight Monica's hold any more. I'm glad she's dead, and once the funeral's over we're going to set a wedding date. Monica's legend is not going to control us."

The door opened on the tail of her tirade. It was Marcus, "What are you all shouting about?" he said, looking concerned.

Eleanor turned to him, calm now and smiling. "Nothing darling, we were just talking. I did tell Allison that we are going to get married as soon as we can."

He turned to me, seeming to seek approval. I stood and kissed his cheek. "It's a good idea, Marcus. It's been a long time. You and Eleanor should set up your own home, run the farm together and have your own life. There's no longer a reason to wait." Marcus was worried that everyone would disapprove, that there would be something indecent marrying so soon after Monica's death. They had been together so long, I felt sure that most people wouldn't notice the change in their status. Eleanor was a strong woman and would be good for Marcus.

I was upset by Eleanor's vision of Monica's destructiveness. Some of it was probably true, and I tried to balance her bitterness with my own feelings for Monica. Was the Monica I had loved and revered all these years just a figment of my imagination? I hoped for all of us that it wasn't.

Emotionally drained I was ready to go back to Snowsdown. I took Marcus' car and left Jennifer and Marcus to be driven back later by Eleanor or Nicholas. Eleanor and I were shy with each other as we said our good nights. We had made some emotional connection for the first time and both felt that we were at the beginning of some understanding of each other.

It was dark driving back. There were no lights on the country roads, so I had a few minutes of isolation from any family demands. I wanted to drive all night alone in the dark, away from Snowsdown and Monica's funeral. But I was going to London tomorrow and needed an early start. I wanted proof that Monica and Carey were Jennifer's parents.

Snowsdown was quiet, everyone seemed to be in bed. There was a light on in the hallway and as I turned it off and began to climb the stairs, I saw that there was a light shining under the library door. Before I could open the door to turn it off, it flew open and Caroline rushed through shouting over her shoulder, "I hated your mother." She saw me, halted for a moment and then pushed past looking wild and flushed as if she'd been crying. I walked into the library and found Colin sitting on the couch with tears streaming down his face.

"She said Mother didn't care about us," he said, "that she'd convinced Aunt Willow that she wasn't smart enough for university, that finishing school was the right place for her. She hated Mother." He was hurt and stunned and we sat together on the couch as he talked about the things Caroline had screamed at him, about their childhoods and all the things Monica had made them do for what she called their own good, never listening to what they might want.

"Most of us feel that way about our parents at some time," I said. "They're the most powerful figures in our lives."

Colin's eyes were dry now and he looked at me. "It's more than that. Caroline said she's always hated it here as long as she can remember. She hated the way Aunt Willow and Uncle Clive treated Mother, that she made them obsequious and then walked all over them. She said that as awful as that was it was even worse when they were in London because they had no interest, no energy, no ideas or plans of their own, that nothing happened unless they were at Snowsdown."

I could believe it, and for the first time felt some sympathy and understanding for Caroline. Willow was a doormat. That Caroline had retained any sense of herself, any fire, no matter how bitter it seemed, spoke well of her. Maybe I should invite her to Connecticut to stay for a few months, to get her away from Willow, give her some freedom. It might not be too late to break through her cynicism. Perhaps we could try.

"And how do you feel about it all, Colin?"

"I don't know—a bit scared, a bit relieved." I must have looked startled. "What I mean Aunt Allison, is, that I'm scared when I think of Mother not being here. She's always explained what to do, where to go, what to study. She even had plans for me to follow in her footsteps as an archeologist." He cast his eyes away, looking embarrassed. "I'm relieved because I don't want to be an archeologist, I want to be a mechanical engineer. I have a devil of a time with Greek." He smiled. "There's a block of some kind."

"Will you be an engineer now, Colin?" I asked. He nodded.

CHAPTER 9

It was barely light when the alarm woke me, and I prepared a cup of coffee to drink as I dressed for my trip to London. I was tapping on Jennifer's door within half an hour. "I'm going to start the car, darling, hurry up." Not wanting to run into Mrs. Potter I went quietly down the stairs, across the hall and around to the garage.

We were borrowing Marcus' car, and Jennifer was soon down to drive me to the station to catch the first train of the day to London. The quietness of the drive, the dewy freshness of the morning, was broken at the station. Jennifer dropped me off and I prepared to join the already long queue at the ticket office.

"I wish you'd tell me what you're up to, Mother."

"I will later, darling, just keep out of everybody's way and avoid answering questions."

She was irritated that I wouldn't tell her exactly what I was going to do.

"I can hardly tell them anything at all." She rolled up the window, put the car in gear and drove off.

The train was crowded with commuters and people going down for the day to shop. It was a two-hour journey and I spent it in the dining car trying to eat some breakfast and drinking lots of coffee. I was going to check Jennifer's birth records at Somerset House; all records of births and deaths were kept there and it should be easy to check their files. There had been no reason to check it before— John and I had accepted everything Monica had told us. I was anxious now to find proof of her birth, although I wasn't sure what I was going to do when I had it. Still surging around my mind was how I would tell Jennifer and John. What was our legal position? Had we really adopted her or was it some farce perpetrated by Monica which she'd thought would never come to light? Perhaps Somerset House could tell me that too.

The train pulled into Euston Station and I forged through the crowds toward the taxi stand. Although I was anxious to move ahead I found myself slowing as I walked across the station. As a young girl I'd taken so many trains to London and I loved the big, old Victorian stations, the glass ceilings, iron girders and the way the light shone through into all the activity. As everyone else who remembered steam engines, I missed them too, they had given the stations a character, and although they were much cleaner now, they weren't nearly so romantic.

It was rush hour, the traffic in London overwhelming, and I thought what a mistake I'd made to arrive at 9:30 in the morning. The taxi eased its way through the center of London toward the Strand and Somerset House. Perhaps when all this was over John, Jennifer and I could spend a few days here together. It was lovely and invigorating and Snowsdown seemed so far away.

I had been to Somerset House once before, when I was thirteen years old—on a school outing with fifteen other girls from Leamington Spa. I remembered that it was once the site of a royal residence and that the current building had been erected as the first modern government offices in the year of the American Revolution, 1776. It looked as Victorian as most other large structures in the city tend to look.

Walking in without the security of my classmates and the assurance of our teachers was much more formidable. It was huge and hushed and everybody else seemed to know exactly where they were going, how to find anything. I approached the receptionist and was directed to the records of births which took me down endless corridors and several flights of stairs to another receptionist. It turned out to be amazingly easy. I stated my purpose, the year of Jennifer's birth, the place which I guessed to be Dunster, Somerset. That was where Monica had taken us.

"What name?" asked the clerk.

"Cartwright or Sherbourne, I'm not sure," I said wondering whether Monica had used her name or Carey's. If Jennifer's birth was legally recorded it had to be under one of them, or possibly both. Surely she wouldn't have falsified the records or avoided them altogether. The clerk completed a form and placed it in a pneumatic tube to swoosh off somewhere into the bowels of the building where the records could be found. I sat down to wait. It took less than five minutes for the tube to return, and I moved to the desk and was handed a copy of a birth certificate: When and Where Born: 9.3.48, Dunster, Somerset. Name if any: Jennifer. Sex: Girl. Name and Surname of Father was blank. Name and Maiden Surname of Mother: Monica Sherbourne. Rank or Profession of Father was blank. Signature and Residence of Informant: Monica Sherbourne, Snowsdown Manor, Lower Pershing, Warwickshire. When Registered: 9.9.48. My hands shook as I read it.

It was one thing to have pieced it all together from Carey's conversation, it was another to see the final proof in black and white here at Somerset House. Mother—Monica Sherbourne. Mother! I hated Monica for her game. She'd fooled us all these years; John and I had been so anxious, so gullible. What papers had we signed in Dunster? I knew why she went there to have her illegitimate baby—it was a place she knew well but where few people would remember her. She used to talk about Dunster and the childhood summers she'd spent there working in a riding stable. When, as children we'd all ridden around on Dolly, Monica always claimed to be a good horsewoman as a result of her summers grooming horses, giving lessons to younger children and being paid with free riding time. None of us had seen Monica on a horse, but she had fond memories of riding.

I went back to the clerk. "Is there any way I can find out about adoptions here?" I asked.

There was but it was much more complicated than getting a copy of a birth certificate. With the protection for parents and children surrounding official adoption it was impossible to find out what I had to know. Were John and I Jennifer's legal parents? I didn't know how to find out.

We had driven to Dunster with Monica. Arriving late in the afternoon, we checked in at a local hotel and Monica took us to see Jennifer who was being taken care of by an elderly woman Monica seemed to know well. The next morning she took us to a local solicitor's office where we were greeted kindly and asked to sign several forms. Jennifer had been so adorable, so lovely, that there was absolutely no doubt in our minds that we wanted her. We signed the forms readily. They were adoption froms the solicitor told us, and I remember John glancing at them without much interest. We were anxious to be on our way with our new daughter. And now we had absolutely no record that it had ever happened. Monica must have, somewhere she must have kept a copy of those forms we'd signed. And as I recalled, she'd signed them too. I had to talk to her solicitor, and if he didn't know anything, I'd tear Snowsdown apart until I did find some proof that Jennifer was ours. Jennifer belonged to us. She was our daughter, not Monica's. The undercurrents at Snowsdown, her desire to have Jennifer there this summer, even her death, seemed to be tied up with Jennifer's birth, the mystery that had surrounded it all these years, Monica's will. The funeral was tomorrow, then the will would be read. There didn't seem to be time enough to sort it all out.

I left Somerset House subdued. The taxi moved through the traffic easily this time and soon deposited me at the station. There wasn't a train for an hour, so I sat frustrated in the station cafe drinking coffee, going through everything that had happened, over and over in my mind. For the first time I thought of Monica and how she must have felt knowing that Jennifer was her daughter, a baby that she'd given up to live in America. Although it was hard to imagine, I could believe that it had all seemed impossible to her at the time. She must have been appalled when she discovered she was pregnant, that her summer love affair with Carey, a married man, her neighbor in England, had resulted in pregnancy. If it happened to a woman like Monica today, she might have an abortion. Twenty years ago, a staunch supporter of the Church of England, it would not have crossed Monica's mind. She couldn't keep the baby; she was going to marry Roger, continue her career. She couldn't tell Carey. Not only was he married to Jessica, she didn't want to marry him. The only thing was secrecy and adoption. How lucky she must have felt to have a sister like me. And until now it had all worked. Was it guilt that had set her on the path to exposure, this ridiculous treasure hunt to show us all the truth? What a cruel, painful thing to do to all of us—and most especially to Jennifer. Sitting there in the railway station I began to wonder whether Monica had started to believe her own press, that she could do anything she wanted, that she was infallible. I wished that it had never started, that she'd kept her secret and died with it.

I arrived back at Snowsdown to walk into chaos. There were no taxis waiting in Evesham and I'd taken the local bus, which, stopping in every village along the way, had taken an hour to reach Lower Pershing. The walk from the village to Snowsdown was a good twenty minutes; all I wanted at that point was to sit down with a cup of tea. Jennifer came running down the driveway to meet me.

"We've had burglars," she cried. "They've torn some of the rooms apart."

We ran into the house together. "Look at the library." She caught me by the arm and led me into a room destroyed. I stood, horrified. All the books had been torn down from the shelves, hundreds of them scattered and torn around the room. Chairs were knocked over, plants scattered across the floor. The clock above the mantelpiece was in thousands of pieces, its face still intact, bizarre and calm in the midst of destruction.

"All the bedrooms were searched too. Roger asked us all to take inventory to see what is missing."

Jennifer was scared, I could feel it in her voice. "Where is everyone, darling," I asked. "When did all this happen?"

I felt helpless looking around the room and walked out into the hallway, closing the door behind me as Jennifer said, "We're all to meet in the drawing room. Roger said we should when we've checked to see what is gone." She didn't answer my question, insisting that we gather in the drawing room as Roger had suggested.

They were all there, Clive, Roger, Marcus, Caroline and Colin. I was greeted by Willow. "So where were you all day?" crying, accusing.

"It seems that we've all been out, Willow. Where was everybody when the burglars were here?"

Roger was pale and shaken, standing before the fireplace, a pad and pencil in his hands. "Allison, I'm making a list. Have you looked to see if anything's missing from your room?"

"I've just walked in, Roger. I'll look in a minute. What were they looking for, what have you all lost?"

Everyone was quiet and for an instant we looked like a pleasant family party about to play parlor games. Nothing in this room had been disturbed, it was comfortable and gracious as always, the late afternoon light filtering through the windows wrapping us all in its warmth.

"Have you called the police?"

Everyone looked to Roger to answer. He was awkward.

"No, I haven't. It doesn't look as if anything's been taken."

"But all this," I waved my hands in the general direction of the library, the rooms upstairs.

Marcus crossed the room to Roger. "I don't care whether anything was stolen, we should call the police. Somebody's been here and wrecked our home. They should be found and locked up." His face was red and angry as he glared around the room. "I'll call them myself."

Roger restrained him. "Not yet, Marcus. Let Allison check her room first, then let's see."

I started for the door. Willow and Marcus moved as if to join me, "No, I'll go by myself."

I wanted to get away from all of them for a minute, to gain some equilibrium. Before opening my own door I peered into Jennifer's room. The bedclothes were strewn around, the mattress tipped off the bed, drawers and their contents from the dressing table tossed aside, books torn down from their shelves. Marcus' room was the same; so was Roger's, Willow's, Colin's and Caroline's. The door to Monica's room was closed but when I opened it the view was the same; chaos. I stepped across smashed bottles, paintings, and bedclothes over toward the bookcase. The books were scattered around the room and I pushed some aside with my foot wondering where the photographs of Jennifer were. There were snapshots of Roger and Monica standing in front of the house, Marcus sitting in his car, Colin going off to school, but none of Jennifer. I turned toward my own room.

Tentatively, I opened the door. There was something behind it, and I had to push hard to force it open. It looked like all the others. I stood in the doorway and looked at the jumble, the confusion, the madness of it all. I began to cry, silent tears running down my cheeks. I didn't have many of my own things here any more, but it was my past that had been torn up and the accumulation of anger, fear and sorrow of the last few days overwhelmed me. I almost closed the door without going into the room but something about the bed held my attention.

The bare mattress was on the frame and sitting squarely on it at the head of the bed was a pillow with something resting in the middle of it. Compelled by the vision of order in the center of such chaos, I moved toward the bed, kicking aside books and blankets and broken glass as I went. I stopped at the side of the bed and gazed down at a neat arrangement of my worst nightmare. It was a blown-up, color snapshot of Jennifer on the beach. I remembered taking it about five years ago in Southampton, and I didn't remember sending Monica a copy. Jennifer was standing on the beach with her back to the sun. I knew she was squinting into the light, her head was tilted to one side. But now I couldn't see her face, it was covered by a splayed, delicate, dead field mouse which was skewered into the photograph and into the pillow beneath it by Monica's pearl-tipped hat pin. Blood from the battered body of the mouse had trickled onto the white pillow. I stared and stared, brought out of my stunned reverie by the sound of my own retching. I raced to the bathroom and afterward lay for a few minutes with my head against the cool porcelain bathtub.

This was not an isolated act of vandalism; it was an indication that there was something wicked happening in this house, to me, to Jennifer. Without more thought I got up from the bathroom floor, cleaned my teeth, washed my face and went back into the bedroom to destroy the evidence. I tore up the picture into a dozen pieces and flushed them down the lavatory with the mouse. I washed the blood stain from the pillow slip and hid the hat pin in the lapel of my dressing gown which was hanging behind the door.

"There doesn't seem to be anything missing," I told the others, who had seemed not to move in my absence. "I don't think you should call the police, Roger."

"Why on earth not, Allison?" Marcus was furious. "This is ridiculous."

No one else said anything but all looked to Roger, who seemed to understand my point-of-view—at least the one I offered. "The funeral's tomorrow, the house is going to be full of people, it's going to be difficult enough as it is without the police all over the place. And none of us think anything is missing."

"And," said Caroline, "old Selby's going to read the will." She sat on the arm of her father's chair, leg swinging. Clive blustered indignantly, "Now, now, Caroline, that's the least of our worries."

"If you ask me," she said standing, "it's our number-one priority."

"Oh, cut it out, Caroline. Aunt Allison's right, the police are the last thing we need at Mother's funeral."

"Allison's right," chimed in Willow. "Nothing is missing." She smoothed her skirt as she stood up. "I suggest we all do the best we can with our rooms and join together to put the library into some order, we'll be using it tomorrow."

"Before we all go off on the cleaning detail, Willow, I'd like to know how anybody got into the house and had enough time to do the damage they did," I said.

Everybody sat down again and I, still feeling sick to my stomach, fixed myself a strong drink and tried to calm down.

"You're awfully pale, Allison," Willow fluttered. "We're all here together, it'll all be all right."

I ignored her platitudinous non sequitur and waited to find out where everybody had spent the day. We pinned it down that the house must have been empty between twelve-thirty and two o'clock. Jennifer and Marcus lunched at Carey's, Colin had gone to The Bell, Caroline was riding, Clive had driven into Evesham for lunch with a colleague, Willow had been shopping in the village while Mrs. Potter had gone home to feed her husband his lunch and Roger was at the Vicarage arranging the service.

"And where were you, Allison?" asked Roger.

"Didn't Jennifer tell you? I needed to get away for the day so I went to London to shop, but I didn't find anything I wanted. I got bored and came home early."

"There's no need to go rushing off to London to shop," Willow defended local merchants, "Evesham has some very fine stores."

"I know, Willow, but I needed to be away, that's all."

Our first task was the library. It took an hour's concentrated effort on everyone's part to put the books back in some semblance of order. The mess of my own room seemed too much to deal with but a sandwich and coffee helped and I put it in order without too much thought. The drawers were back in place, the bed made, *that* pillow stuffed in the back of the closet, clothes hung, drawers back and almost all the books returned to their shelves when Jennifer came in. I looked at her disheveled appearance and remembered what my own day had been about, that I had a copy of her real birth certificate in my purse. I couldn't talk to her now, I needed time to think.

"How was lunch today?" I asked.

"It was lovely. Carey is so charming, I really like him. Nicholas too."

I continued to pick things up. "Weren't Marcus and Eleanor there too?" I asked.

"For a while, then Marcus had to see some of the men and Eleanor needed to do something with the horses. They left after a while."

She wandered around my room, picking things up, putting them down. I became irritated. "Stop that, Jennifer. If you're going to help, do it properly."

"I'm sorry, Mother, but I can't stand it here. Let's go."

"We will, Jen, after the funeral. It's been a miserable time. How about asking Daddy to join us in London instead of here? I looked at her, thinking of how exciting the City had looked today.

She liked the idea and we talked of things to see and what we might do together. I had to make some reservations, and cable John about our change in plans. Perhaps after a couple of weeks away from Snowsdown we could all come back together, briefly. It could never be the same without Monica, it wouldn't be the summer we'd planned.

"I'm going to lie down for a while, dear. I'll be down for dinner." She left and I lay on the bed and tried to think things through.

Sherbourne's Folly

Someone had torn this house apart. Jennifer, Nicholas and Carey were together for a couple of hours. Willow had gone to the village, but she was by herself and could have stayed at the house, Colin was at The Bell but would have had plenty of time for a sandwich, a beer and tearing the house apart. Clive was in Evesham; Caroline, riding; Roger at the Vicarage. Marcus and Eleanor had left Carey's. There had been time for everyone to come back. I floundered in the maze of my family, loving them all, finding it impossible to think of any of them as genuinely crazy. And whoever searched and tore and ripped our rooms apart, had been crazy.

It all stemmed from Monica—Jennifer's birth, the inheritance. What difference did it make if anyone found a copy of the will, Selby was going to read it tomorrow. A later will, perhaps. The elaborate treasure hunt. Monica wanted Jennifer to know about her birth but couldn't tell her openly. Had the knowledge of her leukemia, her death, changed her mind, given her the desire to acknowledge Jennifer as hers? To tell Carey, me, Jennifer, Colin, all of us. Jennifer's clue, what could it tell? Carey's told him he had a daughter, that Monica had borne his child. Carey and Jennifer had both talked to Monica at the Folly, been given clues. No one else had gone that far in the hunt, would their clues have been different? Jennifer's clue:

> For you the race is almost won
> Rest not but go where rest is done
> There volumes can tell you much
> And gates will open at your touch.

I knew what it meant. My mind stopped moving in circles, focused on the clue. I knew what it meant. Monica, ghosts, secret passages. It was in Jennifer's room, stupid, stupid, stupid. Of course, the secret passage. I leaped from bed and raced to Jennifer's room. I knocked at the door. There was silence so I went in. She'd done a good job straightening her room. The books were back in shelves and somehow I had to find the key to open the passage behind the bookcase. It looked like any other wooden bookcase, plain oak, no design or elaborate pattern. It was dark when Monica and I struggled here but I remembered that a section of the bookcase had been swung open into the room, a door to the passage. There were two three-foot units. It had to be the right-hand section—if the left swung out into the room it would hit the foot of the bed. It took no more than five minutes to find the catch on the second shelf from the top of the left-hand side. I pressed what felt like a knot of wood and the bookcase swung slowly into the room. It was dark, I didn't have a lamp, and it was close to dinner time. I pushed it back in place, planning to return later.

The Cartwrights came over and we were all conscious of Monica's absence. Carey kept looking at Jennifer and seemed sad. Nicholas was quietly attentive to her and Eleanor withdrawn from all of us. Willow kept sighing and Clive patted her hand in comfort.

"We're going down to the church after dinner, Allison, to see Monica." Roger asked if I wanted to join them. The coffin would be closed after they left.

"I can't, Roger." I had seen her in Evesham and I

couldn't stand it again. I felt ashamed. No one said anything to me, although I felt Willow's disapproval.

"I'm going too, Mother, do you mind? I want to say good-by."

"No, Jen, I've said my farewell to Monica. I'd rather stay here by myself."

"You don't mind being here alone, Allison?" asked Marcus. "I'll stay with you if you like." Eleanor took his hand.

"Marcus, I've stayed in this house by myself before. I'll lock the doors."

Eventually, they all left and I was alone. I took a flashlight from the hall closet and went back to Jennifer's room. It was dark but I went immediately to the bookcase. It swung back and I turned on the flashlight, to be confronted by a two-foot-square landing and a flight of stairs going down into the darkness on the left. They were narrow and straight and I climbed down backward, slowly, until there were no more steps. Turning my back to the stairs, I flashed the light into the space before me. It was a small room, a table, four chairs, an oil lamp. There was an ancient rug on the wooden floor, the walls were built of rough-hewn planks of wood. Off to the right was another door. I opened it and shone the light into a narrow passageway. I'd explore that later, but first the table. On it was a long manila envelope. It was sealed and addressed to Miss Jennifer Van Dyck. I sat down, rested the lamp on the table and without any qualms, opened it. It was a letter in Monica's handwriting which began, "My dearest Jennifer." I put it aside for a moment and looked at the rest of the papers: "The Last Will and Testament of Monica Sherbourne Dayer-Smith." Turning the pages quickly I saw that it was dated a month ago. Monica *had* made a new will! I began to read it, looking for bequests, to see whether Jennifer was named. I was so absorbed I didn't hear the sounds of someone else in the room with me. The light was knocked from the table. As I twisted around something hard and heavy hit the side of my head and shoulder and then a hand grabbed the will from my hand. I struggled, trying to fight off my attacker. Stunned, I couldn't sense anything of the person fighting for the papers, but the gloved hands felt determined and powerful. The papers were ripped from my hands and as I managed to turn on the chair it fell from beneath me. I kicked out and hit bone. I heard an exclamation, movement and the figure was gone. Not up the stairs but through the door I'd seen on the other side of the room. It slammed and I rushed to open it but couldn't see in the blackness surrounding and smothering me. The footsteps pounded off, away from me. I dropped to my hands and knees, found the flashlight, broken, and beside it a sheet of paper. I picked it up and made my way back to the steps.

Back in my own room, the bookcase closed, panting and frightened I looked at myself in the mirror. I was wide-eyed, pale, covered in black dust. And in my hand the one thing the intruder had dropped, Monica's letter to Jennifer. I moved to sit in the chair and again caught sight of myself in the mirror. Filthy. Opening the door of my room I listened carefully to any sounds from below. The others were back, I could hear their voices wafting up from the drawing room. I closed the door, locked it and moved to

Sherbourne's Folly

the bathroom. Putting the lid of the john down, I sat on it and read the letter. It was dated the day before our arrival.

My dearest Jennifer,

I gave birth to you on September 3, 1948 in Dunster, Somerset. Your father, my lover, was Carrington Cartwright. Our affair began in Greece and we fell very much in love. Maggie and John Davis were a figment of my imagination, the protection I thought I was giving myself, your parents and you.

Soon you will be here again. The last time was just before your parents took you to live in America and I married Roger.

It had been my intention to retain the fiction of Maggie Davis, to die with the truth that was all mine. But now I am dying, it will be soon, and I can't die without claiming you, acknowledging my role in your life. I do this knowing you might hate me, that the family will be pained and angry and that it is a very selfish thing that I do. And yet I hope everyone, and you especially, will forgive me, and remember me with love.

You will say that I rejected you, that I didn't love you, that I loved my own life, my ambition more. What is true is that I was afraid *of changing my life. You would have forced me to make different decisions, and I couldn't. I gave you to my sister Allison, the strong, good member of our family, and her husband, John. They would not be afraid and would always go forward to do what was right and honest. I admire your mother and love her and know that she loves you as a mother does.*

I am telling you this now because I am dying. When

you've read this letter I would like to feel that you can talk to me. I don't want to take your mother's place. How could I? I want to face you squarely with the knowledge of our relationship, to be loved in spite of it, because of it.

With this letter is a copy of my new will. I shall file a copy with Mr. Selby within the next week.

You will be here soon. I am excited and frightened but must do what seems necessary to me now. I do love you, my dearest daughter.

Your Mother,
Monica Sherbourne

I folded the letter and put it under the carpet beneath the leg of the bed where no one would find it and wondered how I was going to tell Jennifer. I had to show her the letter. I had to find the new will.

CHAPTER 10

Monica's funeral was calm and stately. Later the BBC showed highlights on the evening news—family and dignitaries arriving and, after the service, the coffin carried by Roger, Marcus, Carey and three of her colleagues to the grave which had been dug the day before in the churchyard. Sections of the eulogy given by the eminent archeologist Sir Roger Throckmorton were recorded in the background, "Monica Sherbourne embodied the best of humanity—curiosity, tenacity, humor and generosity." The small Norman church was too small to accommodate the hundreds of people who came to the funeral; a loudspeaker system had been set up for those standing outside. The whole village was dominated by the somberness of the occasion, the voices of the Vicar and the eulogists echoing around the village streets. The local school and all the shops were closed for the day.

My own state was one of fear and confusion. I had spent the night pursued by demons, huge field mice bounding after Jennifer as she ran through dark narrow passages trying to escape their pointed white teeth. They didn't catch her—I'd awakened moaning each time it seemed that she would be caught and devoured. I stood at Monica's funeral and wondered whether she could have been murdered. There were reasons to want her dead. Whoever tried to push Monica downstairs, hit Jennifer on the back of the head, wrecked our rooms yesterday, fought with me in the dark secret room last night was probably crazed enough to kill Monica. The coroner said she died of a heart attack; there was no proof of anything else. She'd had a recent history of heart attacks, there were no marks on her body, her doctor wasn't surprised. Wyndham was at the funeral and I was determined to try and talk with him at the house afterward when everyone returned to offer their condolences to the family. If Monica had been killed, we were burying the evidence.

Roger sat on my right. We were in the family pew. The church was dominated by our presence—not only the present but the past. The Sherbournes had been giving windows and monuments to St. Andrew's since the family took over in 1801. The Poyntons had been here as long as the church—which was built in 1154—but their presence in this place was almost obliterated. The early Sherbournes had been anxious to become a great family immediately and had spent a lot of money trying to do it.

Roger was stony-faced and dazed by the proceedings. Never a gregarious man, he had receded further into his own thoughts since Monica's death. Before we left the house this morning he'd asked me, "I did do the right thing didn't I, Allison? I didn't want the police tramping through the house, spoiling Monica's funeral." Falsely, I agreed that he had been right. I didn't want the police called in either because I didn't know what was going on, only that the destruction yesterday wasn't an isolated incident by local vandals. If the police came to investigate, I would have been compelled to talk about the other strange things going on at Snowsdown, about Jennifer's birth. In spite of it all, I still held faint hopes that nothing was seriously wrong, that it was my imagination, that it would all go away. Bringing the police in would have confronted me with a reality I couldn't deal with right now.

Marcus, sitting on the other side of Roger, was furious that we hadn't called the police. "I'm going to," he'd said again this morning. "It's crazy, something vicious happened in our home and you all want to ignore it."

He'd been restrained by Eleanor who brought a rational head to the situation. "Marcus, it might already be too late," she said. "You've all cleaned up your rooms, it's hard to tell that anything happened. If I were the police, I'd be very suspicious."

Marcus agreed but thought it was wrong not to report that the house had been broken into.

"You can do that after the funeral, Marcus," I said. "There's no point in creating any more chaos right now." Reluctantly he'd gone along with us.

Willow had been totally uninterested in our discussion about the police. She was dressed in her best black and, except for her hands, which were methodically shredding a white, lace handkerchief, she seemed perfectly calm. She and Caroline had argued before coming to the funeral. Their voices had rung through the house until Clive, who rarely spoke and never raised his voice, took them each by an arm and said through clenched teeth, "At least have some respect," forcing them off into different cars for the ride to the church. The argument was about money, Monica's money. Caroline wanted to travel around Europe.

"We can't afford it," said Willow horrified.

"You'll be inheriting from Aunt Monica. It won't be that expensive. Why can't I go?"

"Let's not talk about it now, Caroline." Willow turned to get into the car.

"You've talked about it for years," shouted Caroline. "You'll get your share, you can afford to let me go."

Colin, Jennifer, Nicholas, Caroline and Eleanor sat in front of us. Caroline, looking tragically wonderful in her black suit, sat like granite, totally unbending in front of her mother. Later, on the news, we were to see that Caroline's beauty had been captured in practically every frame of the film shot by the BBC. Colin and Jennifer held hands throughout the service, comforting each other. Colin and Jennifer, brother and sister. I had to tell Jennifer, and soon. And everyone else. What about the will? Did Selby have a copy of the latest one, the one torn from my hands last night? I didn't think so. I had to find it.

The richness of the service, the real pain of Monica's death, gave some respite from the doubts and confusions in my mind. I think we were all lulled by memories of Monica and, emerging into the sunshine after the service, everyone seemed much calmer. Watching the coffin lowered into the ground, Roger's handful of soil, the familiar words of the prayers, was strangely comforting. We were linked together by blood and time and would continue. Our tears were sorrowful and releasing.

It was noon before the service ended and two hundred people gathered their cars or found rides to follow the family back to Snowsdown. I rode with Willow, Marcus and Roger. We sat silently as our car moved sedately through the village streets. Local people stood in groups along the

Sherbourne's Folly

sides of the roads and the men took off their hats. Most of them knew us well, especially Monica and Marcus who'd lived in the village all their lives. Many of those people who had worked with the family came back to the house. Many more of the guests were friends and business associates of Monica's. They were the other side of her life, those who knew her as an archeologist, a scholar. Mrs. Potter and several of her relatives had prepared sandwiches and now, dressed in black uniforms, circulated with trays offering sherry and food to those who'd come to pay their last respects to Monica. It began as a subdued affair but spirits picked up as people became involved in conversations and managed to juggle sandwiches, sherry and cigarettes. Except for Roger, who went to rest in his room, the family stayed to talk with friends of Monica's and distant relatives we hadn't seen since Father's funeral ten years before.

I found Dr. Wyndham sitting in a corner by himself, with a plate full of sandwiches on his lap and a glass of sherry.

"Excuse me, Allison." He was embarrassed to be caught wolfing sandwiches and sitting down to do it. "I'm starving, and I thought I'd take the chance to sit for a while and gather my thoughts."

He moved to stand up. "Stay there, Dr. Wyndham, I'll join you," I said pulling over another chair.

"Were you surprised when Monica died, Dr. Wyndham?" I sipped my own sherry and waited for him to swallow his last sandwich.

"Well, sudden death is surprising. And it was sudden," he said. "Why do you ask?"

"When I arrived Monica told me she had leukemia."

He was startled. "But she told me she didn't want anyone to know, and I didn't tell anyone, although I did talk to Roger after her death."

"I know," I said.

"Even when she fell over in the Folly and then down the stairs I kept it to myself. I begged her to let me tell Roger then, but she wouldn't hear of it."

"Did she have heart attacks those two times?" I asked, already knowing the answer.

"Yes," he said, "but very mild ones. I've known people live for years having heart attacks like that. My grandmother had heart attacks for over twenty years, every time more than six people gathered for dinner at our house on Sundays. She died at the age of ninety-seven last year, alone in her own home."

"Why would Monica suddenly have such a massive attack? Would leukemia be a contributing factor?" While Dr. Wyndham sat in thought for a moment I called to Mrs. Potter's niece to bring us more sherry.

"No, leukemia wouldn't be a factor," he said, "except that she was weaker and had had two mild heart attacks before the big one. It could have been something simple that startled her—an unexpected clap of thunder, for instance. But then there wasn't any thunder on Saturday, was there?"

"But she did die, Dr. Wyndham."

"I'm sorry, my dear, that I don't know what happened. I can do no more than guess."

I wanted to ask him about murder. Was there some way in which Monica could have been killed as she sat in the Folly, some undetectable way? But I couldn't ask him without arousing his suspicion, especially as he seemed so sure that it had all been quite natural. On the information supplied by Wyndham, the coroner had looked for heart attack as the cause of death. He'd found that she'd had a massive one and death was duly recorded as such. If someone in the family had hurried along her death in some way, it would have happened before she had time to be frightened. Recognizing any of us she would have smiled and welcomed our cleverness in finding the clues so quickly. There were no unexplained marks on her body, or the coroner would have found them. The contents of her stomach were examined as routine procedure, and no strange substances had been found. I had to find someone besides Wyndham to ask about possibilities.

"You look wiped out, Mother." It was Jennifer kneading my shoulders.

"That feels wonderful."

"Your neck is full of knots, you should probably rest for a while."

"No, I want to stay. I know I couldn't relax anyway." I smiled at her and stood up to try and find something to eat. I too was starving.

"Don't forget, Jennifer, we're all supposed to gather in the library at four o'clock for the reading of the will. We should all be there."

She went off with Nicholas and I wondered what to do about finding a copy of the will that had been taken from me last night. I couldn't go back into the passage right now, there were too many people around, it would take too long and I'd be missed. I was sure that the will wasn't there, but I wanted to know where the passage led, to find some clues to what had been happening. I decided to sneak upstairs and check out the bedrooms. Everyone but Roger was here with the guests, Willow and Clive, Marcus, Caroline, Colin looking pale standing with Eleanor and Carey, Jennifer and Nicholas having an animated conversation by the french windows. I went toward them.

"I've changed my mind. I will lie down for a while, Jennifer. I'll be down in an hour. Take care of her, Nicholas."

"I will, Mrs. Van Dyck. I think we'll walk around the grounds for a while. We'll be back in time."

I was relieved that he would stay with her. The image of the mouse skewered with Monica's hat pin was strong in my mind. It was a warning not to be ignored. I think the dead mouse, more than anything, convinced me that someone here, in my family, was capable of murder: Monica had been murdered and I, on behalf of Jennifer, had been warned.

It was quiet upstairs and I stood for a moment trying to calm the beating of my guilty heart. What would I say if someone found me creeping around in other people's rooms? Roger had said he would be resting in his room. I listened at his door and, hearing nothing, pushed it open. He was sitting in a chair beside the bed, head thrown back, quiet snores whistling through his mouth. I closed the door gently, feeling relieved that he was resting and probably wouldn't wake to hear me moving about. Marcus' room was across the hall. It was a jumble of boyhood souvenirs: trophies from schools, memorabilia of a man who spent his life on the land, pictures of prize animals, and trade journals. His bedside table held a photograph of Eleanor which had been taken a few years ago. She was sitting on a fence, smiling into the camera. How would she feel when she knew Jennifer was her half sister? Her knowledge of her father's and Monica's affair ended with its dissolution; that a child had resulted would be a shock. She'd been hurt and angry with Carey's unfaithfulness to her mother, I hoped she wouldn't be too bitter and even more hurt when she learned about Jennifer.

Willow and Clive shared a large, sunny room which Willow kept immaculate, and Mrs. Potter was forced to vacuum and polish every day. The twin beds were separated by a night table which held a lamp and a photograph of Caroline. The few books in the room were neatly arranged in shelves. Every other surface was bare; there were no pictures, hairbrushes, lotions, any of the odds and ends that accumulate as they please. I was amazed at my skill and calm in rifling through the dressing table and chest of drawers. Jennifer's birthright was at stake, and there wasn't much time before Selby read whichever will he had last received from Monica. I had to find the latest one. Damn Monica and her machinations. She was responsible for this madness directed against Jennifer. It was easy to look through Willow's belongings, to open each drawer and run my fingers around the edges, beneath and between the layers of clothes. They were all empty of papers that could be hidden in the folds of lingerie. The solid desk was locked, and pulling and yanking at the drawers had no effect, there wasn't a rattle or a wobble. I tugged hard and the desk began to move away from the wall, the leather-bound blotter on its top beginning to slide toward the floor. As I pushed it back I saw that it covered something taped to the top of the desk. Moving the blotter completely to one side I saw four photographs taped to the surface of the desk: Colin when he was still at Eton; Caroline staring into the camera wearing a ball gown, Eleanor sitting on a horse; and Jennifer on the beach; a smaller copy of the same photograph that had been pinned to my pillow yesterday. Putting the blotter back, I left the room. There was no reason why Willow and Clive shouldn't have family photographs but why were they under the blotter? I would ask Willow where she had come across that photograph of Jennifer, and if she knew of other copies.

I spent less than two minutes in Caroline's and Colin's rooms. They were both chaotic and looked pretty much as if they had never been cleaned up. Their concession to yesterday's search had been to put books back on shelves. Caroline's room was full of beautiful clothes strewn over chairs, bed and floor. Her dressing table was covered with bottles of creams, perfumes and make-up of all kinds. The drawers were empty. Her bedside reading was Proust's *Swann's Way*, the only thing in her room to give me pause. Colin's room was dominated by gym equipment and some kind of engine parts strewn around the floor. There were no books and no papers.

Frustrated, and still worried, I returned to the drawing room to find that most of the mourners had left. It was three-thirty and in half an hour we were to meet with Selby and hear the will. For the moment there was nothing more I could do. I would have to wait and see.

It was a straightforward will, but the wrong one. We met promptly at four o'clock in the library and Selby was sitting behind Monica's small writing desk. Carey and

Eleanor were invited and nodded awkwardly to us as they walked in. When we were all gathered and facing him, Selby proceeded to speak on behalf of Monica.

He began by offering condolences and talking about his long and pleasant association with her. "As you know," he continued, "Monica Sherbourne Dayer-Smith held your family monies in trust, as they were entrusted to her. With her death that trust may be broken, the monies and land are to be shared among you. Because Snowsdown is your family home it is written in the will that it so continue, that you and your families shall have access to it as long as you choose."

At this he looked down at the will held in his hands and proceeded to read the conditions. To Marcus, with stipulation that until his death Roger would continue to enjoy the house, his home, and the fruits of the land, went Snowsdown. I was surprised, it seemed more likely to have gone to Colin. He was also to inherit all lands and holdings to own, run and profit by as he saw fit. Willow and I were each to inherit one hundred thousand pounds each, and the right to live at Snowsdown if we chose. Colin was to receive the capital, which if liquidated amounted to almost a million pounds. There was a gasp from all of us, we had no idea the trust was so healthy. "To my dearest husband I leave all the royalties and rights to which I am entitled for my books and films, and, of course, the right to Snowsdown as long as he lives and the care of our family." There were smaller bequests to distant relatives, Mrs. Potter, several libraries and the English school in Athens. To Carey, "my dear friend" she left her collection of Greek vases, "to keep or sell" as he saw fit. It was an extremely rare collection, not one to be given out of a family lightly. Carey sat immobile as he heard Selby's words and the surprised reactions of his neighbors. Eleanor made the first overture I had ever seen her make to her father. She took his hand and continued looking ahead toward Selby. Caroline and Jennifer were not mentioned at all.

I was to be an executor. Later I asked Hubert Selby why, what help could I be living in America. "Monica trusted you, Allison. You have your own life, and you see things clearer than if you were here all the time. We can work it out."

"Do you think this was her final will," I asked innocently. "What happens if another one turns up?"

He was horrified by my thought. "I'd be very surprised. If by some remote chance this wasn't the last Will and Testament the new one, with this, would be taken to court and decided upon by a judge. If proof could be given that the second will was the last will, then it would be so awarded." He smiled, relieving his tone. "But it would have to happen fairly quickly. Tax assessment will begin right away, and once that's determined the monies and land will be distributed. Actually, it will take some time, Monica's fortune was enormous." He looked puzzled suddenly, as he looked at me, "Why? Do you suspect there is another will?"

"No," I said without a qualm. "Just curious. Monica mentioned a couple of times that she was thinking of preparing a new one, that's all."

"Oh, well, I wouldn't worry then. This one seems very fair to everyone."

And indeed, the family was pleased with the resolution

of the will. No more trust, no more control. I was concerned that Roger might feel slighted by its terms, since by comparison to Marcus or Colin he had received so little. "No, no, Allison. Monica and I discussed it all long ago. She's left me far more income than I need, there's a steady and sizable income from royalties. I'm happy that I will live at Snowsdown as I have for so many years." He smiled quietly. "What pleases me most is that Monica asked that I take care of the family." Shrugging, his smile became a laugh and for a moment he looked more like the old Roger, warm and loving the way he was before the strain of Monica's death. "I know you can all take care of yourselves, but it's good to know that there's someone to talk to, that home is still here."

Willow was very pleased with it all. She had money and, more important, Snowsdown was still her home. "There's only one thing, I can't believe that Monica didn't mention Caroline in the will," she moaned. "Leaving those Greek vases to Carey, doesn't seem right to me. They're worth a lot of money."

She didn't see Carey behind her. "I won't sell them, of course," he smiled at Willow. "I'll have a safe cabinet built in my house and keep them where I can see them. When I die I shall probably bequeath them to a museum." He seemed unsure of our reactions to his plan.

"That sounds great, Carey," Marcus shook his hand. "Monica loved you like family, and I think it's only right that you should have something that's not only worth a lot of money but which she personally valued highly."

Roger agreed. "They gave her a very special joy," he said.

"Sometimes she would just sit and look at them, a smile and a faraway look in her eyes."

Selby left and everyone made plans for a quiet evening. I made plans with myself to explore the secret passage. The contentment was going to be wiped off all those faces. Monica's will was generous to us all, except that it ignored Jennifer's relationship to her. If she hadn't wanted it known, she should not have started her silly games. It was too late to try and hide it; someone knew, someone had used that knowledge to frighten—perhaps kill—Monica, and to threaten Jennifer. I couldn't ignore it, I couldn't let the horrors just slide away.

CHAPTER 11

It was quite late when I entered Jennifer's room to open the passage. Claiming exhaustion, I'd excused myself from the others to go to bed. Jennifer was out with Nicholas for the evening, and as I opened my own door to listen to the sounds of the house, I heard voices drifting up from the drawing room where everyone was sitting and talking. I wasn't worried about being discovered. Once the bookcase swung back and I was on the stairs, I would close it behind me. The passage obviously led somewhere—wherever my attacker had gone.

Monica's clue for Jennifer had been right for her. It had led me to the letter and the will. Jennifer hadn't told anyone else her clue. I'd told Carey, but I didn't think it was he who had attacked me last night. Someone had followed my movements, someone was watching. Whoever put the mouse and photograph on the pillow had warned me, and I'd ignored it. Now I felt fairly confident that the danger was past. The will had been read, everyone had inherited well. Whoever had the second will believed that it was well hidden, that there was no danger of anybody finding it. I hoped it hadn't been destroyed. I wasn't fighting for Jennifer to inherit any of the estate, but I wanted her established as Monica's daughter. If I didn't tell Jennifer about it all now, someone, some day, might find it necessary to tell her, and I wanted her armed with the knowledge before anybody could hurt her with it. I was used to the idea but still dreaded telling her and John, and seeing the reaction of the family. It would certainly change the image they all had of Monica. And Carey, how would he react when it became general knowledge? But I couldn't worry about any of them; only Jennifer.

The stairwell was pitch black when I pulled the bookcase closed behind me and shone the lamp down the steep stairs. I swung the light around the small, wooden room at the foot of the stairs, picked up the chair I'd knocked over during the fight and looked to see if my attacker had dropped anything that might be a clue to his identity. The room was bare but for the table and chair, and I quickly moved to the door leading into the passage. Stepping through I closed it behind me. The passage, narrow and dark, stretched ahead. It was low and closed and roughly supported by hand-hewn beams and supports. It was damp and dank and I moved quickly forward, along a dirt path, seeing ahead only as far as the beam from the lamp would reach.

Suddenly, the passage divided—left and right. Which way should I go? I swung the beam of light down to the left but couldn't see to the end. To the right, up ahead, was another stairway. I moved toward it, shining the light up its treads, which were dusty but there were still faint imprints of footsteps. I climbed to the top to be confronted by a blank, wooden wall that looked exactly like the back of the bookcase leading into Jennifer's room. I didn't know where it would open, but I pulled the handle to the right and watched as it slowly moved open. It was dark beyond the door but the light of the moon shining through the window showed me that I was in Monica's room. I didn't enter but pulled the bookcase behind me and went down the stairs to try the other passage.

It was much longer, seeming to go on and on and still I couldn't see the end. I had lost all sense of direction, I couldn't tell where the passage might be taking me. I only knew that it was too far to still be running under the house and that I would not emerge into any of its rooms. If these passages had been installed during the civil war when Royalists needed hiding places, it would be reasonable to assume that escape should lead away from the house and far enough away that the Roundheads couldn't readily fan out to encompass the area.

It took fifteen minutes to reach the end. This time there was no stairway to climb but the passage became steeper, loose stones crumbling under my feet as I panted and pushed my way forward. And then the cool of night air coming from ahead, getting stronger and sweeter as I moved on, finally confronting a heavy door. I grasped the knob, turned it and pulled the door toward me to step out into the night. The lamp showed only bushes and trees, crowding in upon me. I looked up and couldn't see the sky. I felt claustrophobic, feeling my breath coming in short, strangled gasps, and I fought to control myself and get my bearings. Turning off the lamp I let my eyes adjust to the dark. Turning from side to side, ahead and then upward I saw above me the roof of the Folly, our Parthenon. Breathing a sigh of relief, I laughed. All these years, right here and we'd never known about the passage or the secret room. Like all children we talked of secret places, asking

Father and Monica about the possibility of some at Snowsdown, but they'd denied the existence of such romantic fantasies. Why hadn't they told us? What fun we could have had playing here. I looked to find a way out of the bushes and into the clearing ahead of me, toward the Folly.

I broke through a well-established path. The bushes had been pushed aside many times, their thickness was an illusion, the branches sprung aside easily. As I walked toward the Folly the moon broke out from behind clouds and streamed down onto the whiteness of this silly, magnificent structure. Monica's furniture was waiting, glowing white from the blackness surrounding it. All was quiet but for the trees and bushes rustling, whispering. The scene was compelling and I climbed the steps to be in the middle of it for a while, to sit in Monica's chair. I looked at the small table in front of me. It wasn't empty. Sitting in the middle of it, held by a heavy stone, was the will I was looking for. I didn't touch it but sat as relief turned to fear as I realized that someone must have been expecting me. I sat and waited and listened, too immobilized by the unknown to grab the will and run out of the maze and back to the house.

And then, from the back of the Folly, out of the shadows, came the voice.

"I have to kill you, Allison, you wouldn't leave well enough alone, would you?"

It was Willow, my sister Willow, stepping toward me with a gun held in her left hand pointing at me. She was dressed for the night, a black sweater and slacks, gloves, a dark hat to hide her light hair. But the voice, that was Willow, quiet and edgy. She stared at me, the gun steady in her hand. It was the look I'd seen the night Monica was pushed down stairs. But this time I couldn't turn to slap her in the face, bringing her back to reality.

I sat ready to leap, my hands clutching the arms of the chair. "Why, Willow? What?" I could barely speak. I couldn't believe it. Willow, quiet, patient, irritating Willow standing before me with a gun aimed at my chest. "What difference does it make, there's enough money and security for all of us."

"You haven't read the new will properly, Allison." She spat out the words, "Monica left everything to Colin and Jennifer, to continue the trust, to minister the money, to control our lives just as she did. I won't have it, I tell you, I won't." She moved toward me and I cowered back into the chair, tensing my body to fight her off.

"Don't move," she said. "You can't get away."

"Why, Willow, please tell me why? You killed Monica, why, why?" I cried.

"I hated her, hated what she did to my life, to Caroline's. You were all right, off in America, the favorite with her bastard daughter. Who was she to order me about, who was she to hand out my rightful inheritance as if she was doing me a favor? I've hated her as long as I can remember, but I killed her, and she's never going to control anything again."

I was stunned by the hate in her voice, the venom spitting out to me in her physical appearance. Gone was the shy, retiring sister. In her place a taut, strong body ready to spring, to explode.

"You had it cushy." She was almost screeching now, but the pitch of her voice was low. "You were in America.

Marcus was all right too. He had the land. But Caroline and I were poor relations treated like dirt under her feet. But she wasn't so wonderful, she had your bastard and she's not going to control my life any more."

"How did you know, Willow? What difference does it make?" I was almost crying, fighting not to, to stay in control, watching for her to give me a split second when I could knock the gun away.

"I found the adoption papers when I found the passage from Monica's room years ago. How do you think I've ever known anything? I've made it my business to know things. I know everybody's secrets."

"Why did you wait?" Keep her talking, keep watching, try to get her off guard.

"As long as Monica didn't acknowledge Jennifer, it was all right. When you came, when Monica forced you to come early, when I knew she had leukemia." She saw my look of surprise. "Oh, I knew. I heard Wyndham talking with her, but leukemia wasn't fast enough when I thought she might make a death-bed confession and change her will. So I killed her." She laughed and it was bizarre, her pleasure ringing through the Folly. "She took a lot of killing too, stupid old woman." She came closer to me. "And I'm going to kill you too. You weren't very clever. You could have left it all alone, gone back to America, taken your brat with you. But, no, you couldn't stop, could you? Stupid."

"Willow, you can't, the gun will be heard, they'll know I was murdered." Keep her occupied, keep talking. Please somebody come. They won't, it's the middle of the night in the middle of nowhere, we're too far away, keep talking, don't let her stop, let her boast. "How did you kill Monica? They said it was a heart attack."

Again, that laugh. "Doctors can be stupid too. I killed her with this, or maybe I scared her to death with it?" She held up something in her right hand. It took a moment for me to see it. Then the moon slipped out from behind the clouds and a beam caught and captured light, from Monica's hat pin, the one that had held the mouse on Jennifer's photograph, the one I'd put in the lapel of my dressing gown.

"Stupid, Allison, right there in the lapel. Easy." Pleased with herself. "It goes in very easy," she gloated, right in the base of the neck and up into the brain. It won't hurt at all. Just a prick and then, nothing."

Again, she moved. If I reached out I could touch her. I glanced at the gleaming weapon raised in her right hand. Her look followed mine. I had my split second and I leaped from the chair which clattered behind me as I knocked Willow to the ground. I heard the gun fall to the tiled floor and didn't wait to see where it went. I ran. Away from the Folly, into the bushes, away, away from this madness, crying as I went, asking for help. Willow was behind me, "You won't get away, Allison. I have the gun." Racing with fear, I listened to crashing branches, my breath coming in short, jagged gasps. I tripped and fell and it was quiet all around me. Where was Willow? Listening. I held my breath. Again there was movement, the sound of running feet on dry underbrush, the snapping of twigs and branches. "I hear you, Allison, I'm almost there." Willow's voice echoed in the canyons of the maze. I didn't know which way to turn, where to run, how to get away. I turned to another path and began blindly to run, my feet getting surer as they crossed the ground and then the hedges opened up and I was back at the clearing, the Folly towering over me. I'd run in a circle and in front of me was my sister, quite mad, waving her gun, "I will kill you, Allison."

"They'll get you, Willow, you won't get away, they'll hang you."

"No they won't. No one knows we're here. They won't be able to prove a thing."

With the confidence born of madness she held the gun forward and prepared to pull the trigger. But now, behind her, two figures appeared. Nicholas and Jennifer were creeping forward, fanning out to each side of her.

"I'll know, Aunt Willow."

Stunned, Willow spun to stare at Jennifer. "You little bastard, how did you get here?" She leveled the gun again. "Move closer to your mother; you'll die together." Nicholas was edging closer. She hadn't heard him and she kept her attention on Jennifer as she moved slowly toward me. And then he jumped at her back, his hand gripping her arm at the wrist, trying to force her to drop the gun. But she held on and began to scream, her cries keening in the clear night air. Jennifer and I joined the struggle with Nicholas. Her strength was incredible as we struggled together. Finally, Nicholas yanked her arm behind her back and, exhausted, defeated, she dropped the gun. She stood perfectly still, her eyes glazed, and there was no response when I looked into her face and used her name.

"We must take her to the house and call the police," said Nicholas. "Allison, you take her arm and lead her. Jennifer and I will walk behind with the gun. I don't think she'll try to get away. I don't think she can."

"The will, Jennifer, get the will," I pointed to the table and she ran to bring it to me.

"How did you get here," I turned to ask as we began our strange procession back to Snowsdown.

"I went to my room, Mother, to get a sweater. The bookcase was open. I fetched Nicholas and we followed you."

Thank God, thank God, I prayed as we walked, Willow's arm cold in my hand, I hadn't closed the bookcase properly. Patient Willow again, shoulders bowed, the acquiescent little sister. So much passion, so much hate.

I viewed the rest of the night through a protective haze. The lights of Snowsdown, the fear and sorrow of Roger, of everyone. Clive breaking down and Caroline looking as if she'd been kicked in the stomach by a wild horse. The police and their questions which I answered quite clearly and calmly, the ambulance taking Willow away, all viewed through a tunnel. Everything else at one end, me here, safe, not feeling, not thinking. Just let it all be over soon. Hold on, it'll go away. They'll leave you alone soon. Just one more question, "Oh yes, the hat pin. Where's the hat pin?" Send a policeman to find it. And Jennifer. I had to tell Jennifer. The will, where was the will? I had it safe in my pocket, tomorrow I would think about it, talk to Jennifer, try to understand that my little sister Willow had killed Monica, would have killed me and Jennifer, had enough hate to kill all of us, had enough demons to drive her to madness.

I went to bed and passed into oblivion.

CHAPTER 12

Telling Jennifer that Monica and Carey were her real parents was the most difficult thing I've ever done in my life. She had come to my room early, opening the door quietly. "Come in, Jennifer, I'm awake and about to get up." Oblivion had turned into restlessness and I had lain awake for what seemed like hours, tossing and turning, frightened, worried, stunned.

"I've fixed some coffee, Mother. Shall I bring you some?"

"No, I'll be downstairs in ten minutes." This was it, no more delays. I dressed quickly and joined her in the dining room remembering my last conversation here, with Monica. She had been wrong about things not being irrevocable; the fact of Jennifer's parentage, Monica's death, these things were not irrevocable.

Jennifer was tired and subdued. We both were. Willow and her removal from Snowsdown were uppermost in our minds.

"What happened, Mother, I don't understand."

Where to begin? Jennifer knew only what she'd witnessed in the maze last night. She knew nothing of the events leading up to it.

"Last night was just the end of things, Jennifer. It began twenty years ago in Greece." I stopped, thinking for a moment that it had really started when Willow, Marcus and I were children under Monica's authority. That was when things became twisted for Willow, when she began to hate.

"What do you mean, Greece, twenty years ago?"

"Monica was there on a dig, Carey went on business, and they fell in love."

"What does that have to do with Aunt Willow trying to kill us last night?" she asked.

"They had an affair, Jennifer, and Monica became pregnant. She didn't tell Carey, or anyone." She looked puzzled, not understanding. I didn't know how to make the information less painful for her. "You were the child she had, Jennifer. Monica and Carey are your real parents."

She sat immobile across from me, her face ashen. I made no move to touch her, I just watched her carefully. "And then what happened?" The words came painfully from her lips.

And I told her how she had become our daughter, about Monica's secret which she'd kept all these years, even from me and John, how desperately we'd wanted her and accepted the story of Maggie Davis.

"When did you find out, Mother? When?" It seemed important to her, my answer. I was glad that I could tell her truthfully, "Just recently, from things Carey said, the accidents happening, the discontent everyone felt in the air with Monica and the treasure hunt. Lots of things. I confirmed it two days ago when I went to London and checked the records of your birth."

"Why didn't you tell me right away? You could have." Accusing, not sure.

"Because I didn't know what was happening, Jen, and I

was frightened that if you knew then you wouldn't be safe."

We were silent together for a moment and then she got up from her chair and came around the table to hold me. "It'll be all right, Mother. It just takes a little while to sink in. I feel as if I've been hit over the head." Her sudden grin was wry. "At least now I know I do belong to this family." She sat down again and we talked about the will, Monica's death and what would happen to Willow.

"You know, darling, the new will makes a difference. You and Colin will share everything equally, and it could change your life dramatically. It will be a responsibility that might be difficult to assume," I pointed out. "For one thing, you should live in England if you're controlling the trust."

"I don't want it," she said vehemently. "What's wrong with the first will? That seems much fairer to me. Can't we destroy the new one?"

She made my heart sing. This new will was a vicious, narrow one, basically the same as the one Father had written which had given Monica control over the lives of everyone. Much better that the trust be broken, the monies and land split fairly, giving us all freedom to lead our own lives.

"I agree with you, Jennifer, but we'll have to talk to the others, especially Colin. Perhaps we'll never tell Selby about it, we'll destroy it."

"It's going to be hard to keep it quiet," she pointed out. "There has to be some logic, however misguided, for Aunt Willow to have murdered Monica and then try it on us."

"We can try," I said standing and holding out my hand to Jennifer. "Let's go and call Daddy. I want him to come and fetch us right away." I missed John desperately, I needed his support and comfort, right now. "And then we'll talk to the others together. Okay, darling?"

As hard as it was to tell Jennifer about her parents, it was much harder to tell the others. Perhaps because of the way we sat together, broken and sorrowful, blank faces, staring at each other in wonder. And somehow now, being totally unable to react to any new information. None of us knew how to relate to each other any more. The news of Jennifer's birth threw familiar relationships off base. I thought though that with time that would pass and we would go back to our comfortable, familiar manner with one another.

Monica's body was exhumed that same day for another autopsy. Fortunately, the grave had not yet been filled in and it was a fairly simple matter for the police to have the coffin raised and taken off to Evesham again. It was removed before dawn, and done so efficiently that the local people had no idea that it had happened. The cemetery was blocked off for the day and the story spread that new grass sods were to be laid. By nightfall Monica's body was back in the coffin in its grave and buried. The coroner's report was surprising. Monica *had* died of a massive heart attack. There was a pin prick at the base of her neck but hardly deep enough to draw blood. It was also impossible, even if Willow had inserted the hat pin deeply enough, to kill Monica that way. But Willow thought she had killed Monica with the hat pin. Whether she had caused the heart attack was open to speculation; we would never know.

Willow was under observation in the psychiatric wing of

a hospital in Birmingham. We didn't know whether she would be declared insane, but she was now in a catatonic trance. Clive and Marcus had spent the day there, sitting with Willow. She didn't know them or respond to anything. She just stared blankly ahead of her looking nowhere, or at her private visions. They were both shaken when they returned to Snowsdown, Clive overwhelmed by the state of his wife, this new knowledge of parts of her he'd never suspected before, "She looked so old, shriveled, a shadow. It wasn't Willow."

Jennifer asked me to go with her to see Carey, and we walked across the fields in the bright sunshine.

"It's funny, I've never ever wanted to know who my parents were," she said. "You and Daddy were who I wanted. I couldn't imagine being part of other people." She smiled. "It's not so bad. I don't think I'll ever think of either Monica or Carey as my parents, but I'm glad they're both special people." She turned to me, asking, "They are, aren't they, Mother?" I nodded, "You know how I've always loved them, especially Monica, and that hasn't changed."

She linked her arm through mine. "We do have the same blood now," she said grinning. "You really are my mother."

I felt wonderful as she talked, and wondered how much my fear of losing her love had encouraged me to delay telling her the truth. But now it didn't matter, and my heart was lightened as we walked and talked and I tried to explain why I thought Monica had hidden her birth from Carey. Suddenly, I remembered the letter Monica had written, still hidden in my room.

"Darling, forgive me. Monica wrote you a letter. So much has happened, I can't believe it slipped my mind." I tried to repeat what it said. "Shall we go back and get it, Jen? I'm sorry."

"No, it'll be there when we get back, let's get on to Carey's now, Mother."

He was expecting us, having received today's news from Eleanor. As we walked up the path to his house the door opened and he stood there, waiting. Jennifer left me and walked into his arms. He held her for a minute, kissed the top of her head, then led us both inside.

We went into the sitting room where Eleanor and Nicholas were waiting. It was difficult, none of us quite knowing what to say. Eleanor finally came toward Jennifer about to shake her hand but suddenly, laughing, kissed her cheek and said, "Welcome, sister." We all laughed with her and relaxed together.

"It's all going to take a bit of getting used to," Carey said looking worried.

"Don't worry, Carey." Jennifer turned to look at him. "I don't think things will change much, just a slight readjustment of certain knowledge. I hope we'll like it, but I don't think it will change our lives. And anyway"—she turned to glare at all of us—"my father lives in America."

Carey put his arm around her shoulder and, unable to say anything, kissed the side of her head.

Eleanor seemed more at ease than anyone. It surprised me because I'd worried that she would be most upset by Jennifer's relationship to her father. She'd adored Carey when she was a little girl, and it would be hard to share that love with a half sister suddenly thrust onto the scene.

But she was happy, she and Marcus were getting married and, it was true, things wouldn't change very much. She almost seemed to enjoy the idea of a younger half sister.

We talked about Willow, speculating on the reasons behind it all. I didn't mention the second will, wanting first to talk with the others about our joint decision—perhaps we would never mention it. I hoped we could destroy it and go on as if it had not existed. But Carey would have questions, and perhaps they would have to be answered.

Carey wanted to talk about Monica. "We were very much in love with each other once," he said. "And we never did stop loving each other. I loved Jessica, my wife, too," he said, turning to Eleanor. "She was always my soul. But Greece has a different reality, and Monica and I were there together. It was overwhelming for both of us, I think. I suppose what I really want to say is that you were both children born of love," and he embraced both Eleanor and Jennifer with his eyes. And then to Eleanor, "Your mother knew about my love for Monica. I could never keep anything from her, and I didn't want to."

Jessica had known as she lay ill in her bed. Probably she'd known even before Carey told her. Jessica had been every inch—and more—the woman, the legend, that was Monica. That was something Eleanor had never known.

"I promise you, Eleanor, your mother wasn't pained by it. I wish I could explain it to you, but I can't, except that she was free and loving and still embraced me, knowing always that I loved her." He looked at Eleanor, "I love you very much, my darling," and held her close for a moment and then to Jennifer. "And Jennifer's a new joy in my life."

I watched them all and felt very moved by Carey who had led a lonely life—one without someone who was his own—for a long time.

Jennifer and Nicholas left to walk back to Snowsdown. I stayed with Eleanor and Carey for a while, talking about Willow and the way we'd known her. I was full of mixed emotions, relieved that the truth about Jennifer's birth was in the open, still stunned over Willow's transformation and how close both Jennifer and I had been to death. And Monica's death was still painful to look at closely. I knew it would be a long time before I would see the truth of it all; all I could do was to take a little piece at a time, examine it and gradually build up some understanding, some reason why it had all happened. Talking with Eleanor and Carey was part of it. We didn't dwell on recent events but remembered Willow as a child and young woman, retelling family stories which seemed to us to highlight her personality. We laughed over old times and felt stronger for it.

I walked back to Snowsdown alone thinking about John's arrival and how he and Jennifer and I would go away together. I didn't want to stay at Snowsdown any longer, and I didn't think I'd ever want to come back. But as I approached the house and saw the lights welcoming me home again, I knew I wouldn't be able to stay away forever. It was too much a part of me. What I needed was distance, time, to carry on with my own life again in Connecticut.

Jennifer was waiting, "Now can I see the letter, Mother?" I pulled it out from under the rug and handed it to her. She sat for a long time looking at the pages and then I saw the tears streaming down her cheeks. "I'm glad she wrote it, but it makes me feel so sad. She must have been very unhappy."

"I don't think so, darling. At times, perhaps, but she made her own life, and it was a good one. She knew you were loved and safe."

She wiped her eyes and folded the letter putting it away in her pocket in her jeans. "Shouldn't we go and talk to the others about the will?" she asked.

We went downstairs together and found everyone in the library. Clive was sunk into a chair, looking gray and tired. I didn't know what he would do without Willow, they'd always seemed such a perfect pair. He would be very lonely —if she didn't recover, she would be held in a psychiatric hospital somewhere, slowly slipping away, further and further from Clive, further from his hopes.

Caroline would have to lead her own life. It probably wasn't in her nature to be of much comfort to Clive. But perhaps. She was sitting on the arm of his chair, an arm around his shoulder, still elegant but no longer quite so distant. She was strong-minded, and I thought she would work things out and survive well.

Colin walked towards Jennifer as we came into the room. "I agree with you, Jennifer, let's forget this new will. The first one is much more reasonable, and what do we need everything for?" He and Jennifer together looked like brother and sister, sharing a sense of earnestness and intensity. "Do you have it with you?" he turned and asked me. I held it out, and taking it from me he tore it into several pieces.

"Wasn't that a bit hasty, Colin?" I asked. "I thought we were going to discuss all the implications first, not only the legalities, but Willow's condition, her motivation for trying to kill us last night."

Clive stood up. "We were, Allison, but Marcus and I saw Willow today," his voice strained and broke. Caroline came and led him back to his seat and Marcus finished his sentence. "Willow isn't going to recover, Allison, ever. The doctors say that even if she is able to function again, she probably won't remember any of the past. We don't have to explain anything to anyone. Except ourselves."

"It's enough," said Roger. "Let it go."

John arrived the next day. What joy to see his wonderful, confused face. Jennifer and I were packed and ready to go to London immediately. We didn't stay long, only a few days before we traveled back to America by ship. The five days at sea were renewing, refreshing, happy. The prospect of going home to Connecticut was welcome, and I felt ready to look forward to our own lives.

Two letters arrived within the first few days of our arrival. One from Nicholas to Jennifer saying that he'd decided to go to Harvard and that he was eager to see her. The other was from Roger. Caroline had decided to go to the Sorbonne to study French literature, Marcus and Eleanor were married in a civil ceremony, and he and Colin had decided to have the maze and Folly removed from the property—there would no longer be a Sherbourne's Folly, only Snowsdown. It was a letter of good news.